Interesting Places

Matthew Storm

For Clark Fair and Terri Zopf-Schoessler

Who are largely responsible for this

ACKNOWLEDGMENTS

Many thanks to Michele, for reading yet another of my painfully bad drafts.

Also thanks to Helen Jane Long, Keren Ann, Yoko Kanno, Origa, Joe Hisaishi, and Nobuo Uematsu, for the music.

Chapter 1

Dracula was *pissed*.

In hindsight, Oliver Jones would have had to admit that his plan to walk into the vampire lord's castle and politely ask him to stop terrorizing the neighboring Romanian villages probably hadn't been the best idea he'd ever had. Sally Rain had suggested dropping a fuel-air bomb on him from their airplane as they passed by safely overhead. Tyler Jacobsen, Oliver's closest friend on the team, thought a high-powered sniper rifle fired from a safe distance would be a better plan. That way they could verify the kill later and make sure the vampire didn't somehow put himself back together after they'd shredded him. Oliver wasn't sure that vampires could actually reassemble their bodies at will, but to be fair he didn't really know all that much about vampires in the first place. His boss, Artemis, had told them that Dracula was a special case, anyway. She'd claimed that many years ago an earlier lineup of their team had reported that he'd turned into a bat and escaped from them in that form, but Oliver thought she might have been joking. It was very difficult to tell with Artemis.

1

If the bat story was true, though, it made Dracula unique among vampires, and Oliver wanted to get a look at him up close. It wasn't every day you got to meet Dracula, after all. He had wondered if it would be bad form if he asked for an autograph.

"We're really going to just march right in there?" Sally Rain had asked as they approached the castle's front doors. She unsnapped the thigh holsters that held her silver pistols in place. "Maybe you want me to shoot him a few times first and soften him up a little?"

"I'm sure that won't be necessary," Oliver had said. "Why wouldn't he be reasonable when he sees there are three of us and one of him?"

"Because he's freaking *Dracula*?"

But Oliver had insisted on trying diplomacy first, figuring if the vampire gave them any trouble, Tyler could wolf out and put an end to him quickly enough. "Wolf out" was the term Oliver used when Tyler transformed into a hulking seven-foot-tall werewolf. He hadn't come up with a better way to say it, and it wasn't like he could look it up in the dictionary. The transformation into wolf form made Tyler virtually invincible, as far as Oliver was concerned. It made for a good backup strategy.

But their brief meeting with Dracula had gone poorly, and Tyler had barely begun "wolfing out" when the vampire picked him up by the throat and threw him fifty feet into one of the castle's walls. Tyler had been knocked out cold.

Dracula's throne room was a simple affair. There was the ornate throne itself, of course, which appeared to have been carved out of a particularly dense wood, stained until it was nearly black, and then crusted with diamonds and rubies. It sat at one end of the room, perched on a stone dais at the top of half a dozen stairs. A long red carpet led down the stairs and all the way to the main doors on the other end of the room where they'd entered.

Other than the wooden throne and the carpet, the throne room was devoid of any furnishings other than a dozen chandeliers suspended from the stone ceiling, each holding dozens of lit candles. The candles provided more than enough light to see by, but Oliver couldn't help but wonder whose job it was to climb a ladder every day to replace the old candles and light new ones. It wasn't a position he'd have wanted to be in.

He had plenty of time to ponder this, given that Dracula had punched him square in the chest just a moment before, knocking him onto his back several yards away. Oliver wasn't entirely sure he was ever going to be able to get up again.

Still lying on his back, he heard the sound of Sally Rain's twin pistols firing rapidly, and then clicking as the magazines emptied. Oliver managed to look up from his spot on the floor. Dracula appeared entirely unimpressed by the gunfire. Sally's bullets had torn the vampire's white tuxedo shirt and dark vest to shreds, of course; Sally hadn't missed a single shot in all the time Oliver had known her. But the vampire wasn't bleeding, and if he was in any pain at all, he had a fantastic poker face.

Frowning, Sally looked at one of her pistols. "Well, shit."

Oliver got to his knees, trying to think of what to do next. Dracula was just over six feet tall and had superhuman strength, as he'd already demonstrated. His skin was impossibly pale and Oliver might have described him as entirely colorless, save for his bright red lips. He had black hair down to his shoulders that had not been even slightly mussed by their battle, if what had just happened could really be called a battle. Oliver had a pistol tucked away in an ankle holster, but given that guns had so far proven entirely ineffective against the vampire, he wasn't sure how much good that was going to do. Oliver wasn't a particularly good shot, either. He'd been practicing at a firing range since he'd joined the team six months ago, but he still missed his targets as often as he hit them.

"Good god," Tyler's voice came from behind him. Oliver turned his head. Tyler had regained consciousness and crawled to a spot next to him. "I can't believe how much that hurt."

"You okay?"

"No!" Tyler was bleeding from the nose and still had impressions in the skin of his neck left behind by Dracula's fingers.

"Any ideas?"

"I should be able to change form in a minute or two," Tyler said. "I have to catch my breath so I can concentrate. Can't you do *your* thing?"

Oliver knew exactly which *thing* Tyler was referring to. Months ago, Oliver had shown an ability, if that was the right word for it, to manipulate reality. He'd ultimately used the power, under extraordinary circumstances, to annihilate the Kalatari, a race of humanoid lizard people who had been bent on murdering him. But the power hadn't manifested itself since then. Oliver had tried practicing, concentrating on changing small things around him, but had never achieved any results.

He might have been tempted to dismiss the whole episode with the lizards as a crazy dream, except for…

"Hello?" Tyler snapped him out of it. "You wiped out the Kalatari easy, right? How about one vampire? Blast him!"

"I can't!" Oliver protested. "I think the only reason it worked last time is I'd been hit in the head so many times I probably had a concussion." That had been a very long, and often painful, day.

Tyler thought that over for a moment, then hauled back and punched Oliver hard in the face. Oliver went tumbling backwards.

"Ow!" Oliver protested, his head spinning. "What was that for?"

Tyler pulled Oliver up into a sitting position. "Do you have a concussion yet? I can hit you again if you want."

"No!"

Oliver looked back toward Dracula's throne. The vampire had picked up Sally Rain by the throat and was holding her above his head, leering at her. "You do look delicious," Dracula said, "but you're so *strong*. You'd be wasted as a meal. I have much more…*interesting* plans for you."

Sally kicked him. Oliver had been on the wrong end of Sally's physicality before. She was the toughest person he'd ever met, but Dracula didn't even seem to have noticed the impact. He laughed and threw her backwards, where she landed in a heap. She was back on her feet an instant later, holstering one of her pistols at her thigh and then reaching for a spare clip.

Dracula raised one arm and pointed at her. "Come to me,"

he called, his voice suddenly unnaturally resonant. Oliver felt a shudder, and then a warmth filled him as if he'd just swallowed a large shot of tequila. He found himself suddenly wanting to go sit at the vampire's feet, to touch his cape, just to *be* in that wonderful presence. He shook his head and the feeling dissipated as quickly as it had come over him. What the hell had *that* been?

"Did you feel that?" Tyler asked. "I swear to god, I wanted to go make out with him just now."

"It's some kind of mind control," Oliver said, pointing at Sally. "Look!"

Sally's gun and the spare clip had dropped from her hands. Her whole body was stiff, as if she'd been hit with a bolt of electricity. Eyes wide, she took an odd, halting step toward Dracula, her limbs moving like she was a marionette being manipulated by strings.

"Aw, hell," Tyler said. "He's got some kind of sexy power!"

Sally took another step forward. "Go for her gun," Oliver said, drawing his own from the holster strapped to his ankle. "We'll take him together. If we hit him enough times, maybe we can slow him down long enough to grab her and get the hell out of here." It wasn't the best plan Oliver had ever had, but it beat every idea he'd come up with up until now.

At that moment a small, furry blur shot past him, heading straight at the vampire. "Banzai!" Jeffrey yowled.

"Oh, no," Oliver breathed. His cat had arrived.

Jeffrey had been a stray cat that Oliver had taken to feeding back home in San Francisco. At that time Jeffrey had been entirely ordinary, as far as cats went. He'd been on the receiving end of the first manifestation of Oliver's reality-altering power. Jeffrey had been gifted, if that were the right word for it, with the power of speech. He was the reason Oliver could never quite forget the things he was capable of. The cat never stopped reminding him about it.

Jeffrey bounded up the stairs to Dracula's throne, yowling all the way. He launched himself at the vampire's chest and latched on with all four feet, hissing ferociously. That was enough to break whatever mental hold Dracula had over Sally, who slowly shook her head as if waking out of sleep.

Jeffrey slashed at Dracula's face with his claws, leaving a red streak on the vampire's pale white skin. "Take that!" he yelled. "And this!" He slashed the vampire again. Dracula roared, either from pain or annoyance. It was the first time Oliver had seen him react to anything they'd done to him.

"Hey, Oliver!" the cat called, turning his head so he could see better. "I got him!"

"Great," Oliver said.

Jeffrey clawed his way over to Dracula's back as the vampire tried to shake him off. "What do I *do* with him?" he asked, before biting into the back of Dracula's neck.

Oliver got to his feet. "Hang on?" he suggested.

But Dracula had had enough of the cat. He finally got his hands on Jeffrey and hurled him at Oliver. Tyler stepped forward and managed to catch the cat just before he crashed into Oliver's head. "Ow," said Jeffrey.

Dracula turned back to Sally and extended his hand once more. She'd managed to reload her pistols and cover most of the distance to him in the time he'd been distracted, but immediately froze up again, her guns clattering to the ground. Oliver felt the vampire's powerful mind touch his own again. Maybe he should go over and apologize to him? Barging into the great vampire's castle had been so rude, after all. Maybe Dracula would even show him favor and let him live in the castle? Was that too much to hope for?

"Ugh," Tyler said. "I wish he'd stop doing that."

Sally was only a step away from the vampire now. He smiled at her. "My dear, you are so beautiful." He extended his other hand to stroke her red hair, then cupped the back of her neck and pulled her closer.

Sally smiled back at him. "Aw," she said. "You really think so?"

Dracula blinked in surprise. "What…what did you say?"

Sally cocked her head at him. All traces of her being under any kind of control had melted away in an instant. "Moron," she said. "Did you *really* think that was going to work on me?" Then in a blur of motion, one of her hands disappeared into her black leather jacket and emerged an instant later holding a long wooden stake. Before Dracula had a chance to react, she slammed it straight into his heart.

"Ssh," Sally whispered.

The vampire staggered backward, both hands clutching the stake in his chest. He made a noise like a choking donkey and collapsed onto his throne. Oliver saw dark red lines appearing on the skin of the vampire's face and hands. Tendrils of smoke began to rise from them a moment later.

"Sally!" Oliver yelled. "Get away from him!"

"Holy crap!" Jeffrey said. "I didn't see *that* coming." He

struggled his way out of Tyler's arms. "Take that, fangy! Yeah! That's what you get!"

Dracula's body heaved once and then began to crumble, bits of him turning to ash and falling to the floor. Sally stood over him, her eyes gleaming. "You should have listened to Oliver," she said. She prodded what had once been one of the vampire's legs with her boot and the ash gave way, scattering harmlessly on the stone floor. Dracula was no longer a threat to anything but vacuum cleaners. A minute later all that was left of him were his ruined tuxedo and black cape.

Oliver and Tyler joined Sally at the throne. "Well, that was something," Tyler said.

"*Something*," Oliver said.

Sally glanced over at Oliver. "Next time we have to do something like this, we do it *my* way, okay? None of this, 'oh, let's just go talk to him' shit."

"Fine," Oliver said.

"Did you guys see how I was kicking Dracula's ass?" Jeffrey asked.

Sally knelt down and scratched the cat behind the ears. It was the first time Oliver could remember her showing him any kind of affection.

"You know," she said. "I'm actually starting to like you."

Jeffrey purred enthusiastically.

Chapter 2

"I still can't believe he was wearing a cape," Tyler said.

The four of them had waited in Dracula's throne room for long enough to make sure he didn't have the power to reconstitute himself, but after an hour all that had happened was Jeffrey scattering the vampire's ashes from one end of the floor to the other. "Doesn't this look kind of like litter?" he asked after a while, examining a bit of ash stuck to his front paw. "It looks like litter to me." The group left for the airport before the cat had any further ideas on that subject.

They were currently 48,000 feet over the Atlantic Ocean on their way back to San Francisco in a private jet owned by Oliver's new company, The Araneae Group. Oliver tended to think of the vehicle as "the plane," but that didn't really do it justice. The plane resembled a smaller version of the Concorde. About half of its cabin was laid out like a comfortable living room with eight lounge chairs and wooden tables. In the rear there was a bathroom and a room with two twin beds, and in the front was a small kitchen area where simple meals could be prepared. Since Oliver had joined Araneae a small litter box had been put in a corner of the plane for Jeffrey, the cat having loudly complained he shouldn't have to "hold it" when everyone else had a nice bathroom they could use whenever they wanted. Oliver had never actually seen the cat use the box, and he had admitted he preferred his box at home. He just didn't want to be treated like a second-class citizen.

As far as that went, their plane was much like any other overly-fancy corporate jet, except for the fact that it had retractable missile launchers in its wings and was capable of reaching Mach 3 if necessary. Oliver had never seen the plane in combat and hoped he never had to, but he did find the vehicle fascinating. It was one-of-a-kind, as far as he knew. Like many other things he took for granted now, he wondered where it had come from. Neither Tyler nor Sally knew, and Artemis rarely suffered questions. She'd just ask if he didn't have anything better to be doing and go back to sipping her tea.

Sally had put the plane on autopilot and joined them in the cabin. Oliver had once questioned the wisdom of leaving the cockpit unattended during flight, but the computer system that controlled it had been designed by the technical member of their team and was capable of performing most of the functions required for flight by itself, and probably do them better than a human. Sally, the only pilot on the team, had told him that except for takeoffs, landings, and dogfights, she'd just be getting in its way.

"The cape did surprise me," Sally said. "Isn't that from one of your movies? I've never seen anyone actually wear one."

"Dracula always wears a cape in the movies," Tyler nodded.

"It's like a tradition. Lives in a castle, dresses like he's late for a costume party…"

"He looked like a twit," Sally said.

"Is that why his mind power didn't work on you?" Oliver asked. "You were too busy laughing at him in your head?" He and Tyler had been forced to admit they'd both been a bit mesmerized by the vampire's mental power when Sally questioned why neither of them had been more useful during the fight.

Sally shrugged. "I guess I just didn't want to be his girlfriend," she said. "Unlike two people I know." She smirked at Tyler. "You didn't cry when I staked him, did you?"

"Oh, shut up," Tyler said. "I didn't want to be his girlfriend."

"I didn't want to be his girlfriend, either," Jeffrey said. "His sexy powers were no use against me!"

"You were supposed to wait outside," Oliver said to the cat. "I thought I made that pretty clear. 'Jeffrey, wait in the car. Jeffrey, it's too dangerous.' Doesn't seem ambiguous at all."

"It's a good thing for you I came in when I did," Jeffrey said. "Since you were about to be Dracula's girlfriend."

Sally laughed and scratched the cat behind the ears. "You did good."

Oliver's cell phone chirped. He fished it out of his pocket and glanced at the screen. "Artemis," he announced. "She wants an ETA on our landing."

Sally glanced at her watch. "Five hours, at this speed," she said. "I can go up front and open it up if she needs us there sooner."

Oliver typed out a response and sent it to Artemis. A moment later his phone chirped again and he read the reply. "No rush," he said, "but she wants us in the office when we land. Seven picked up some kind of localized electromagnetic storm up near Sausalito and she wants us to check it out."

"What the hell is an electromagnetic storm?" Jeffrey asked.

"I saw that on *Star Trek*," Tyler said. "It's when..." he thought about it, "no, I've got nothing." He suddenly perked up. "Maybe this means we're finally going to meet some aliens!"

Sally frowned. "I think it's just a fancy way of saying it's a strong electromagnetic field," she said. "Lots of things cause that."

"Like what?" Oliver asked.

"Sunspots?"

"Why would we be going to Sausalito to investigate sunspots?"

Sally shrugged. "I don't know. Maybe it's not sunspots. You can ask Seven when we get there. I don't know why he's not checking it out himself, honestly."

Seven was the technical member of their team. Seven wasn't his real name, and Oliver had no idea what his real name actually was. He knew more about computers than anyone Oliver had ever met, and interacted with them in a way that suggested they were not as much tools to him as they were his friends. Oliver wouldn't have been entirely surprised to discover that Seven was actually some advanced form of anthropomorphic computer himself, even though that didn't seem very likely. Then again, six months ago Oliver would never have suspected that one day he'd be keeping company with a talking cat and watching Dracula take a stake through the heart. Life could be very strange sometimes.

"He's probably in one of his agoraphobic phases," Tyler said. "I remember once he didn't leave the office for 369 days."

Oliver blinked. "*369 days*? That's over a year."

Tyler nodded. "I know. It had to be exactly 369 for some reason. I think it had something to do with prime numbers."

Oliver thought that over. "369 isn't a prime number."

"Then I have no idea. Seven's in his own world. I don't think even Artemis knows *why* he does what he does."

"Any idea what we're going to be looking for in Sausalito?" Oliver asked Sally.

"I don't know. Maybe some of those *Star Trek* aliens you two are always going on about. It would be a change of pace, at least. I'm getting pretty sick of vampires and lizard people. I'd be happy with an old-fashioned ghost hunt right about now."

"That's...something you do?" Oliver asked. Artemis had assigned him a stack of case files to read when he'd joined Araneae as a way of providing him an education in what they did. There was very little vocational training available for his current job, after all. He hadn't made much progress on the files, though.

"I haven't, but this one," she nodded at Tyler, "told me some stories."

"Ghost hunts freak me out," Tyler said. "I did one before I

met either of you that was so bad, the guy I worked with back then quit and joined the priesthood afterward."

"Really?" Oliver asked.

Tyler nodded. "And he moved to Cleveland, too."

Jeffrey rolled onto his back and gave an exaggerated wail. "Oh, no! Not *Cleveland*!"

"Be quiet," Oliver said. "What do you know about Cleveland, anyway?"

"It's in Cuyahoga County, for one thing."

Oliver stared at the cat in surprise. "Really?"

"Of course it is. See? I know more about Cleveland than you do!"

Sally stood up. "I'm going to check up front. I'll give you guys a heads-up before we land."

"I think I'll find something to eat," said Tyler, heading for the kitchen.

Jeffrey curled up on Oliver's lap. "And I need a nap after my big fight with Dracula."

Oliver scratched the cat's shoulders and he purred contentedly. "You were very brave," he said.

"Damn right I was," said Jeffrey. And then the cat promptly fell asleep.

Chapter 3

They landed at a small airport just south of San Francisco a little more than five hours later. The sun was beginning to set as they unloaded their gear and piled into a Lincoln town car, again with Sally behind the wheel. The three of them had left their own cars in their office's parking garage before the trip. Artemis preferred they take the Lincoln when they were on "business," if for no better reason than nobody near an airport was likely to give it a second look. There were times that it paid to be inconspicuous, and Artemis was a big proponent of hiding in plain sight.

"Think we have time to get something to eat?" Tyler asked. Oliver suppressed the urge to roll his eyes. Tyler had devoured three meals on their flight back from Romania. Eating was never far from his mind, but somehow he never appeared to gain weight. To Oliver he looked like Shaggy from the old *Scooby-Doo* cartoons, although he didn't recall Shaggy ever wearing a Hawaiian shirt, and Tyler rarely wore anything else. Tyler claimed becoming a werewolf had affected his metabolism, but he never seemed to stop being hungry whether he changed into wolf form or not.

"We should check in at the office first," Sally said. "If Artemis really does want us to hit Sausalito tonight, we'll get something on the way up there."

"What would we even do?" Oliver asked. "Walk around town and look for electromagnetic storms?" He thought that over. "I don't even know what one looks like."

"I have no idea," Sally said. "Seven probably has equipment that can pick them up. Or, I don't know, maybe we'll run into some flying cars. Whatever it is that electromagnetic storms do."

"I want to go home," Jeffrey complained. "I miss my toys, and my bed, and my television…"

"*My* television," Oliver said.

"*Our* television."

"Fine. You didn't have to go to Romania with us, you know."

"I get lonely when you leave me for too long," Jeffrey said. "Then I have to pee on your bed so you understand how sad I was."

Oliver nodded. Last month he'd left the cat behind when Artemis sent him on a trip to South America to look into reports that an ancient temple had somehow disappeared without a trace. The noxious state of his house when he returned home had convinced him never to leave the cat alone again, unless Jeffrey insisted on it. And quite possibly made some kind of recorded statement promising that he'd behave.

Traffic was light on the way into the city. Oliver had lost

track of what day it was thanks to international travel, but his phone's screen told him it was Sunday. Downtown would be quiet, then. The area around their office in the small financial district near the end of Market Street was a hive of activity during the week, but a ghost town on weekends. That was just as well. Oliver didn't feel much like dealing with crowds after their trip, and if they did wind up going to Sausalito tonight, it would be an easy drive. They could be over the Golden Gate Bridge and on the waterfront in half an hour, at most.

The Araneae Group's main office was on the 41st Floor of a skyscraper not terribly far from Oliver's old office. He'd worked as an analyst at a small hedge fund there, and had always assumed he would stay in that job until he retired. That was until one day an assassin posing as a SEC investigator had tried to kill him in one of the hedge fund's conference rooms. Tyler had come to his rescue, shooting the assassin in the head. And then, much to Oliver's surprise, the assassin's wound had healed almost instantly and he'd continued pursuing Oliver, only to abandon the hunt when he was betrayed by his client, one of the lizard people who had wanted him dead. Even if Oliver had wanted to go back to his old life, it would have been very difficult to just pretend none of that had ever happened, however unlikely all of it may have seemed. Artemis had offered him the opportunity to do something new with his life, and he'd taken it.

Now he did a different kind of work entirely, although he wasn't exactly sure how he'd describe it if he were put on the spot. It said "consultant" on his business card, but that could mean almost anything. *Paranormal investigator* might have been a better description for what he actually did. In any case, it wasn't something he could talk about at parties, even if he were invited to a party and actually went, which had not happened in recent memory. The Araneae Group had been legally established as an international competitive intelligence firm, whose business it was to advise clients all over the world. In fact, they had no clients, and as far as Oliver knew they never had. Something would come to Artemis's attention, and she'd send them out to investigate. Money never seemed to change hands. Oliver wasn't sure where their funding came from, but Artemis had deep pockets and connections in extremely high places.

As Oliver had expected, the financial district was nearly deserted when they turned onto Pine Street. "We could hit Chinatown later," Tyler suggested. "Everything down here is going to be already closed."

"I want shrimp," Jeffrey said. "And noodles. Get me some noodles."

"I'm never getting you noodles again," Oliver said. The mess left behind after the cat's first attempt to eat chow mein had required Oliver to hire a professional carpet cleaning company.

"Are you still whining about that?" the cat asked. "I told you to cut them up for me."

"I did cut them up."

"I guess the pieces weren't small enough, were they?"

Sally turned the car into their building's underground parking garage and started down the ramp that led to the lowest level. Like most buildings in the financial district, theirs had little guest parking and nearly all of the spaces were assigned to tenants. The garage was nearly deserted today as a result. The only other vehicle on their level was a rusty old

Econoline van parked near the elevator lobby. That was unusual, Oliver thought. The van must have belonged to a contractor or an employee of the building, but there was no company logo on it. On a weekday, the building's security officers probably would have turned it away at the gate. But come to think of it, Oliver's team hadn't actually come through the gate today.

"That's weird," Oliver said.

"What?" Tyler asked.

"The gate was up." Tyler glanced at him curiously. "The garage gate outside. It was up when we came in." On weekdays, security officers would stand at the garage's entrance, checking IDs and turning away tourists looking for a cheap place to park before they headed off to the Embarcadero to shop. On weekends a full-length metal gate served that purpose, instead. Anyone working on the weekend could enter a code on a panel outside and the gate would roll up, but it rolled back down once a car passed through.

"I guess it was," Tyler said. "I didn't notice before."

Sally pulled the Lincoln into its assigned spot near her Miata. "Maybe we're going to be kidnapped," she said dryly.

Oliver eyed the van. "Well…"

She smirked at him. "Don't worry, Oliver. I'll protect you."

"Me, too," said Jeffrey. "Me and Sally are total badasses. Did you see how we handled Dracula?"

Oliver sighed. "I just thought it was strange the gate was up. That's all."

They got out of the car, Jeffrey hopping down onto the

cool cement of the garage floor. The cat didn't like to be carried, considering it an undignified way to get around. That opinion could change at a moment's notice, though, and it often did. Jeffrey wasn't exactly consistent, but after all, he *was* a cat.

Twenty feet away the glass doors that led to the elevator lobby slid open and Seven stepped into the garage. He had a lean build, circular eyeglasses, and spiky blond hair that seemed to point in every direction. Oliver had assumed the man must use a great deal of hair gel in the morning and had asked about it once, but Seven had replied he'd never used "product" in his life. When Oliver asked why his hair looked like he'd stuck his hand in an electrical socket, Seven had muttered something incomprehensible about humidity and walked away.

Seven wore a white lab coat and held a tablet computer in his hand. He studied it for a moment, a worried expression on his face. "What what *what?*" he muttered to himself.

Sally stopped in her tracks and held up a hand to keep the others from advancing. "What's going on?" she called, her hands drifting toward the thigh holsters that carried her pistols.

Seven tapped the tablet with a finger and frowned. "There was another burst," he said. "Electromagnetic. Strange. Shouldn't be possible in here without..." he trailed off, looking at the van and biting his lip.

"Without what?" Sally asked.

Seven's fingers danced over his tablet. "No," he said. "Not possible. Not here. They're gone. All gone."

"Oliver!" Jeffrey whispered loudly enough for everyone nearby to hear him easily. Quiet whispering was a skill he had yet to develop.

"What?"

The cat nodded at Seven. "I think he's finally lost it."

Seven shook his head. "No, not lost. Not lost." He stared at his tablet for a moment and Oliver saw what little color the man had in his skin drain from his face. "Found. Oh, no. *Found.*"

"Found…what?" Tyler asked.

Seven looked up at Sally. "Run, Sally! Run now!"

The back doors on the Econoline opened and a man slowly emerged, stepping down right next to Seven. Oliver's first thought was that the man looked like he'd wandered off the set where somebody was filming a science fiction movie. He wore a black bodysuit with illuminated strips that ran down his arms and legs. Metallic plating covered his chest, looking like something a motorcycle racer might wear for protection, with similar reinforcements at his knees and elbows. His right eye looked normal enough, but the left one glowed blue, as if it were being lit by a bulb implanted just behind the eyeball.

All that was disconcerting enough by itself, Oliver thought, but the black assault rifle the man held in his arms was even more worrisome.

"Holy shit," Tyler said. "I don't believe it."

"What the hell is that?" Jeffrey screeched.

"Cyborg!" Seven shouted, taking a step away from the man. "Get out of here!"

The cyborg slowly turned his head to look at Seven, moving as if he were exhausted, then raised one fist and backhanded him across the face, sending him sprawling to the ground. He turned back to the others. "Colonel Salera Rain," he said, speaking as if with great effort. He sounded as if he wanted nothing more than to climb into bed and sleep for the next hundred years. As Oliver watched, something sparked on his chest plate and made a noise like a fuse burning out. The cyborg, if that's truly what this was, appeared to be malfunctioning.

Oliver had never actually seen one of the cyborgs before. He'd heard stories from time to time, and he knew he'd undoubtedly learn more if he ever found the time to go through that stack of case files Artemis had given him, but they'd seemed like a fairly low priority. He didn't know the exact circumstances, but Sally had been involved in a conflict with them and claimed to have exterminated their entire race. At times she seemed smug about it, but as Oliver had gotten to know her better he'd started wondering if that was really the case at all. The Sally he knew was as hard as nails and the best fighter he'd ever seen outside of an action movie, but she was far from heartless. However deeply guarded they may have been, she did have feelings.

At the moment, though, she just gaped at the cyborg as it took a step toward them. Oliver couldn't recall ever seeing her rendered speechless before. It was like she'd seen a ghost, or perhaps *all* of the ghosts in the world at once.

"Colonel Salera Rain," the cyborg repeated. "You are guilty of genocide. For this, you are sentenced to death." He raised the assault rifle at her. "Rot in hell, you evil bitch."

That got Sally's attention. She turned and shoved Oliver straight into Tyler, sending them both tumbling down behind the Lincoln. Jeffrey squealed with fear. "Stay down!" Sally commanded. Then she was running away from them, her silver pistols appearing in her hands as if they'd been there all along.

The cyborg opened fire, but rather than bullets, a bolt of blue energy shot out at Sally, just missing her head. It slammed into the cement wall of the parking garage behind her, dissipating into a web of blue tendrils that left a smoking scorch mark on the wall. Still running, Sally returned fire. She was heading for her Miata, Oliver realized. Maybe she intended to drive away and lead the cyborg away from them? Sally wasn't the type to run.

A flurry of Sally's bullets slammed into the cyborg, sending him back a step but not appearing to penetrate his armor. He fired at her again, this time hitting the Miata. Sally rolled behind the car and popped up again an instant later, using it for cover. She let loose another barrage of fire until her guns clicked on empty.

Oliver managed to get his gun out of his ankle holster and fired two shots at the cyborg, missing him entirely. The cyborg turned toward him. "I have no fight with you," he said. "Stay out of this." Then he fired three times at the Lincoln. This time the energy appeared to electrify the car.

"Get back!" Tyler shouted. He, Oliver, and Jeffrey scurried away from the car as the metal began to smoke.

Sally had taken the brief interval the cyborg had been distracted to pop open her Miata's trunk. She came out of it with an AR-15 assault rifle. Sally didn't like to go anywhere without a small arsenal to keep her company. She leveled the rifle at the cyborg and fired six shots. Six 7.62 millimeter bullets tore through the cyborg's chest plate. He managed to get one more shot off but missed wildly, then dropped the rifle and collapsed to his knees.

Sally advanced on the cyborg slowly, the AR-15 pointed directly at his skull. After a moment's hesitation, Oliver and Tyler approached as well. Oliver kept his gun lowered at his side. Even if Oliver had been better at shooting things, he doubted the cyborg had the strength left to reach for his weapon.

Sally stopped three feet away from the cyborg, just out of arm's length, even though it seemed unlikely she was in any danger of him trying to reach for her now. The cyborg took a slow breath and coughed, flecks of blood appearing on his lips. Oliver was amazed the man was still alive at all, but as he watched he could see that the cyborg's armor was slowly stitching itself back together, bits of metal elongating and joining each other, but the process didn't appear to be entirely working. Was he too badly damaged, or was it due to the poor condition he'd seemed to be in when he'd gotten out of the van? And if his armor could rebuild itself, did that mean some similar process might have been working on his internal organs? Was that why he was still breathing?

"I failed," the cyborg said, shaking his head slowly.

"You did," Sally said. "How many of there are you?"

"I was the last," the cyborg said. As Oliver watched, the cyborg's armor slowly stopped repairing itself and he heard a noise like a bank of fluorescent light bulbs being switched off.

"What is your designation?" Sally asked.

"My name is Jonathan," the cyborg said.

"What is your designation?" Sally repeated, louder this time.

"HK-1987-DT."

Sally nodded. "You were a hunter. How many families did you run down? How many people did you kill?"

"Too many," the cyborg said sadly. "I was a hunter, but that was a long time ago. My name is Jonathan."

"Should we be getting a doctor?" Oliver asked.

"No," Sally said.

The cyborg looked up at her. "Why did you kill us?" he asked. His illuminated left eye had gone dead, its power source seemingly terminated. A tear ran down his cheek from the other. "It was *over*. We were cured. We were people again. You didn't have to kill us."

Sally opened her mouth but closed it again. Whatever she'd expected the cyborg to say to her, this clearly hadn't been it. "I couldn't," she finally said. "I just couldn't."

"Couldn't?" the cyborg asked.

"Let you live," she said. "After what you'd done, I just couldn't...we were never going to go back to normal after that. I wanted to, but..." she looked away. "I'm sorry." Then she pulled the trigger on the AR-15, sending a bullet through the cyborg's skull. Bits of brain and tiny pieces of metal splattered onto the cement behind him.

"Jesus *Christ!*" Jeffrey cried.

Sally lowered the gun and sighed heavily.

There was a long silence, and then a familiar voice said, "Well, Sally. I suppose this means now you really *have* killed them all."

Oliver looked up. Artemis had stepped out of the elevator lobby, her arms crossed in front of her. Seven stood just behind her, rubbing at a developing bruise on his temple.

"So...I guess this means we're *not* going to Sausalito?" Tyler asked.

Chapter 4

Roughly half of The Araneae Group's office on the 41st floor looked much like that of any other office one might visit in the financial district. Glass doors led from the elevator lobby into a finely-appointed reception area where framed portraits of major cities hung on the walls. Four large chairs sat around a circular table next to a water cooler. Nearby a two-foot tall snake plant grew out of a white pot. Two orchids sat together on a long L-shaped reception desk.

On a weekday Bruce Caldwell, the firm's receptionist, would have been behind the desk. He normally sat with a Bluetooth receiver in his ear and greeted any visitors who might happen by with a cheerful smile. Bruce was nearly seven feet tall, built like an NFL linebacker, and had a small arsenal tucked away in his desk. To the best of Oliver's knowledge he'd never had the need to use it, or the switch on his phone that would lock the entire place down with steel doors like a bank vault. Oliver found himself wishing Bruce worked weekends; they could have used another pair of strong hands as he and Tyler dragged the dead cyborg's body inside.

Behind the reception desk was what Oliver thought of as the executive area. Eight private offices were connected by a hallway that ran from one end of the building to the other. Only four were currently occupied. Their staff numbers could fluctuate and were hard to predict from one day to another. It wasn't as if they could put up a "help wanted" advertisement. Employees at Araneae typically fell into their positions through circumstances outside their control. Tyler had joined after he'd been turned into a werewolf and found himself unwilling to return to his old job as a police officer in Honolulu. Oliver had been offered a job after his incident with the lizard people. Seven had been recruited from the government. Oliver had assumed he'd worked for the NSA at one point, but Seven had laughed uproariously when Oliver had asked and said something about not being in kindergarten. And Sally...Oliver had never gotten the details on that one. Sally didn't talk much about her past, Artemis didn't talk much at all, and while Tyler knew the story, he'd told Oliver that it wasn't his story to tell.

The executive half of the office also had a large conference room with presentation equipment, a small kitchen area, and a space Oliver called the "crash room." It held two twin beds, a couch, several bookshelves, and an entertainment center. Seven seemed to spend more time staying there than he did at his own home, wherever that was. Oliver had stayed there overnight once or twice when he'd found himself too tired to manage the commute home. He'd brought in a litter box and set of food and water bowls for Jeffrey some time ago, just in case the cat happened to be at the office for some reason. Tonight he was glad he'd done so; it might stave off the cat complaining until they got home.

The other half of the office, accessible only through a set of heavy security doors in case someone managed to get by

Bruce, contained Seven's lab. It was *one* of his labs, anyway. He had at least two others that Oliver knew of in other cities. This one was filled with computers, stacks of servers taller than Oliver, and a variety of technical equipment. Oliver didn't know what half of the things in there did, and wasn't entirely sure that all of them originated on Earth. He'd only been at Araneae for six months, but found very little was capable of surprising him anymore.

A side room contained a small operating theater. It wasn't used for medical purposes, but rather for examination and occasionally disassembly of interesting things they found on their assignments.

"Get him on the table," Artemis said, nodding at the cyborg as they stopped for Seven to enter a security code outside the lab. "Seven, take him apart. I want to know everything about how he got here. The rest of you, when you're done, my office." With that she turned and headed down the hall.

Oliver had never quite gotten used to taking orders from Artemis. It had nothing to do with the fact that she was female, or that Oliver had any interest in being the boss himself. It was rather that Artemis appeared to be a ten-year-old girl. He knew that she wasn't, of course, at least not chronologically. Nobody on the team knew exactly how old Artemis was, and the girl had never volunteered the information, but a very old vampire he'd met once had told him that he'd first met Artemis when he was still very young. Oliver had taken that to mean she could be hundreds of years old, but once in a conversation Artemis had made reference to having had difficulty understanding the intricacies of Roman tax law. It had taken Oliver a moment to realize she wasn't talking about a trip she'd taken to Italy recently.

Oliver and Tyler helped Seven get the cyborg onto the operating table and then walked back to the executive area with Sally.

Artemis was waiting for them behind a large oak desk when they reached her office, fingers steepled in front of her. Four chairs sat in front of the desk. She didn't need to motion for them to sit down. Oliver felt a sense of dread, as if he were being called into the principal's office for a scolding. That seemed strange to him, given that he hadn't actually done anything *wrong*, and also that she was wearing a t-shirt with a Mr. Snuffleupagus print on it, but Artemis tended to be stern on a good day, and this was no longer a good day.

A china teapot sat on a silver tray in front of them, with three small cups next to it. Artemis poured the tea silently. Oliver and Tyler each took a cup. Sally didn't touch hers. She hadn't said a word since putting a bullet in the cyborg's head.

Jeffrey jumped onto Oliver's lap. "I don't see a cup for me," he noted, looking at the tray.

"Have you begun drinking tea?" Artemis asked.

"No, but it's nice to be offered."

"I shall have to remember that." Artemis took a small sip from her cup. "First things first. Are any of you injured?"

Oliver and Tyler shook their heads. "He didn't seem to want to hurt us," Oliver said. "Well, not me and Tyler."

"Or me," said Jeffrey.

"Sally?" Artemis asked.

Sally stared off into space, her eyes vacant. Oliver wasn't

sure she'd heard the question. On second thought, he wasn't entirely sure she even knew where she was.

Tyler put a hand on her arm. "Sally?" he asked gently. "Are you hit?"

Sally looked down at his hand as if confused by the physical contact. "No," she said. Her voice sounded slightly groggy. If she hadn't been in his presence the entire time since they'd encountered the cyborg, Oliver might have thought she'd snuck off to a bar for a quick drink or five.

"There is that much, then," Artemis said. "Someone should tell me what happened now." She looked at them. "Begin speaking."

Sally didn't look to be in any condition to talk, so Oliver took the initiative. "We were just coming back from the airport," he began. It only took a few minutes to break down the encounter. The whole thing had been over nearly as quickly as it had begun. Oliver paused for a moment when he was finished. "I thought the cyborgs were gone," he said to Artemis.

"It would appear that one survived," Artemis noted. "Hopefully he was telling the truth when he said he was alone, but I suppose he had no reason to lie." She pressed a button on her phone to activate the intercom. "Seven?"

"Here," Seven's voice came back.

"Report."

"I've barely started with him!" Seven protested. "Their armor doesn't come off that easily. Half of it is grafted into the skin."

"First impressions."

Seven sighed loudly over the speaker. "He was already badly damaged before Sally shot him. I don't think he'd have lasted for more than a few more days."

"How was he damaged?" Artemis asked. "Had he been in combat?"

"Not recently. I'm running some of his blood now, but I'd say most of his nanobots have been down for a while. I think the virus got him but he managed to survive it."

"How is that possible?"

"No idea. Interference at deployment, maybe. Some kind of corruption. He was running on empty, though. I'm sure of that much."

"He had nowhere to go for repairs," Tyler said. "The rest of them were dead."

"What about Overlord?" Artemis asked.

"Disabled. I doubt it's been active since the end of the war. I'll try to confirm it, but as far as I can tell he was a human, at least mentally."

"Keep working." Artemis ended the call. "We may wind up calling this lucky," she told the others. "One of them was dangerous enough. If six cyborgs had survived, I suspect things would have ended quite differently."

"He said he didn't want to fight me or Tyler," Oliver said. "Why not?"

Artemis watched Sally for a moment. "He didn't come here for a fight, Mr. Jones. He wanted justice, or what he believed to be justice. I imagine it was all he felt he had. There was no place left for him in his world."

"Which makes me wonder how he got here," Tyler said. He glanced at Sally. "Our mirror was broken. Could there be another one?"

"Perhaps, but I suspect he arrived through other means. They had been working on teleportation for some time; perhaps that work finally came to fruition." Artemis ran a hand through her blonde hair. "Seven may be able to tell us more at some point, but I suspect that the electromagnetic storm we picked up in Sausalito and the similar readings in the garage were related to his journey here."

"It took him over a year," Tyler said quietly. "All that time, just to get here and…" he put a hand on Sally's arm. "Well, he didn't get you. You're fine."

Sally was still staring at nothing.

"Sally?" Artemis asked. "Are you all right?"

Sally shook her head. "He…he was a *person*."

"Of course he was a person, Sally. They were *all* people. I did try to tell you that once before, if you remember. At the time you told me to…" Artemis trailed off. "It no longer matters."

"Why did he call you *Salera*?" Oliver asked.

"Because that is her name," Artemis replied.

"It's not my name anymore," Sally said. "Don't say it again."

"Why not?" Jeffrey asked. He looked at Oliver. "Does this mean we can change our names whenever we want? I want everyone to call me Big Jim Sla…"

"Enough," Artemis cut him off. "Tyler, take Sally home

and keep an eye on her tonight. Oliver, stay a moment."

Oliver expected Sally to protest that she didn't need to be taken care of, but she didn't say a word as Tyler helped her to her feet and led her out of the office. To Oliver she looked frail, as if she'd aged fifty years in the last half hour. She moved like she wouldn't have been able to walk, or even stand up, without assistance.

Artemis sipped her tea as she watched them go, then turned back to Oliver. "Well, Mr. Jones. You seem to be having a bit of a day."

"I kicked Dracula's ass," Jeffrey said.

"Did you?" Artemis asked, eyebrows raised. "I was almost certain you would come in handy sooner or later."

"Really?"

"No, not really."

"Meanie."

A faint smile crossed Artemis's lips, and then her neutral expression returned. "Well, then. Where should I begin?"

Chapter 5

Artemis disappeared into the kitchen to make another pot of tea. Oliver sat quietly with Jeffrey for a moment. "I thought things couldn't get any weirder with you people," the cat said, stretching out on Oliver's lap. "Then a robot from the future shows up and tries to kill everyone. I can't even remember what my life was like before I met you."

"You were an ordinary cat before you met me."

"You say *ordinary* like it's an insult."

"It wasn't. Anyway, cyborgs aren't technically robots; they're a combination of human and machine. And I don't think he was from the future."

"Where else would he have come from? I saw a movie once where a robot came from the future and tried to kill this lady, and the police shot him a bunch of times but he didn't care, and in the end he got smashed flat."

"But that was a movie," Oliver pointed out. Artemis entered the office with a fresh teapot. "Movies aren't real life."

"I saw Dracula in a movie and it turned out he was real life, too. He even wore a stupid cape like he did in the movie."

"Was he still wearing that cape?" Artemis asked, taking her seat. "I told him once it made him look like even more of a buffoon than he already was. I imagine I'll have occasion to tell him again."

"Um, we *did* kill him," Oliver said. "Sally staked him and he turned into ash."

"And I scattered him all over the place," Jeffrey said. "I was going to pee on him just to be sure, but then everyone wanted to leave all of a sudden." He looked at Oliver. "See? You should have let me pee on him."

"I assure you that would not have helped," Artemis said. "That one always comes back. Perhaps in a hundred years. I would not worry, Mr. Jones. I doubt you will still be around next time."

Oliver imagined that was supposed to sound reassuring, but given the night's events a reminder of his mortality really wasn't what he'd needed. "And you *will* be around?"

Artemis sipped her tea. "That seems very likely, does it not?"

"How old are you, anyway?" Jeffrey asked. "Are you as old as the hills?" Artemis gave him a cold look. "Ah, never mind," the cat said nervously.

"I didn't teach him that," Oliver said. "Your television privileges are revoked," he told the cat.

"Your sleeping through the night privileges are revoked," the cat said.

"If you're both quite done?" Artemis asked. Oliver nodded. "Very good. Why don't you tell me what you already know? Or what you have surmised?"

"Sally doesn't talk about it," Oliver said. "I'd just be guessing, mostly."

"You are fairly astute, though. Enlighten me."

Oliver took a breath, considering how to put all of this. "Sally is an alien from another galaxy," he said. "Her people fought a war with a race of cyborgs and she used some kind of weapon of mass destruction against them that destroyed their planet, and then she came here to live on Earth for some reason."

"And she's from the future," Jeffrey said.

"She's not from the future," Oliver said.

"But the robots are."

"Cyborgs," Oliver corrected him. "And they're not from the future, either."

Artemis shook her head. "I may have to reconsider what I said before. That was almost entirely wrong."

"Oh," Oliver said.

"Are *you* from the future?" Jeffrey asked Artemis.

"No. Sally is not, in fact, an alien. She is a human, and she is from Earth. However, she is not from *this* Earth. You are familiar with the concept of parallel dimensions?"

Oliver thought it over. "Only in the sense that I've seen them on *Star Trek*."

"He watches a lot of *Star Trek*," Jeffrey said.

"No, I don't."

"You want to be best friends with Captain Picard," the cat said.

"I never said that! I said if I had to choose a captain…"

"Enough," Artemis cut him off. She looked at him sternly. "I seem to recall giving you a rather large stack of files to read, Mr. Jones. At the time I said you might need the information contained within in the future."

"Yeah."

"It would appear that you have neglected that duty, preferring instead to spend your time watching television."

"I haven't read *all* of them," Oliver said, realizing he sounded like he was making excuses for not doing his homework. "There were a lot of them, and we've been busy."

"Plus he has to watch *Star Trek*," Jeffrey said.

Artemis rubbed the bridge of her nose with her fingertips. "Very well. Rather than have you take any further guesses, I will inform you that Sally led a commando team into our world a little more than two years ago."

Oliver nearly gasped. "They were *attacking* us?"

"No. They had discovered a certain artifact on *their* Earth and were attempting to discern what it did. In fact, it was a gateway between worlds."

"The mirror Tyler mentioned before?"

"Indeed. At least you were paying attention to that much. There were two mirrors. One on their Earth, and the other on ours. Fortunately, the mirror in our world was locked away in

Vault 3, so their arrival here went unnoticed to most people. We, of course, noticed immediately."

"I would think so." This was beginning to remind Oliver very much of a plot device he had seen on *Star Trek*. He decided not to mention that to anyone.

"When we made contact with them, Sally asked if we could render them assistance. They had been engaged in a war with the cyborgs for some time, and things were going badly for them."

"Were the cyborgs from the future?" Jeffrey asked.

"No," Artemis said. "They were largely from Milwaukee."

Oliver wasn't sure he had heard that correctly. "They were from *Milwaukee*?"

"Indeed."

"I'm *definitely* going to start reading those files soon," Oliver said. "Maybe I'll take some home."

"You would be wise to educate yourself, but I will give you the quick version. The outbreak, which is how they referred to the cyborg problem, grew out of plague research."

"The *plague*?"

"In their world, the plague killed more people than cancer. It was a rather unpleasant business."

"They should have gotten some cats in there," Jeffrey noted. Oliver stared at him blankly. "To kill the rats," the cat explained. "Rats are bad news."

"It was not carried by rats," Artemis said, "but that is hardly relevant to our discussion. Traditional medical science having failed them for hundreds of years, they eventually developed an alternative cure. It lay in nanotechnology."

"This I know," Oliver said, perking up. "Tiny little robots, right?"

"Quite so. Small enough that thousands could be injected into a human bloodstream, where they could seek out and destroy plague cells. While I am not a physician, I understood enough of their science to see that it was quite brilliant."

"I would think so," Oliver said. "I've read that we're doing research on that kind of thing here, but it's a long way off." He thought it over. "You could cure cancer, heart disease...I mean, if you designed the nanobots right, you could probably have them performing surgery on a cellular level. So what went wrong?"

"Everything," Artemis said. "The nanobots were controlled by an artificial intelligence so that in addition to seeking out plague cells, they could anticipate future mutations and adapt without the need for human intervention. While it had a limited scope, the A.I. was, in a sense, taking the place of a doctor." She sighed. "Unfortunately, it was the A.I. that evolved, rather than the plague cells. It determined that in order to protect itself and its hosts, it needed the power to control the hosts."

"Like if your doctor followed you around telling you what you could eat?" Oliver asked.

"Rather more invasive. The A.I. wrote itself a new program they called Overlord, which it used to take over the host's higher brain functions. And then it determined that in order for the hosts to prosper, it needed to control more of them. To use your analogy, it was like your doctor saying that because cheeseburgers are unhealthy, nobody should be able to eat them at all."

"Okay," Oliver said. "I'm not sure that was the best analogy anymore."

"It was *your* analogy," Artemis said. "In any case, those who carried the nanobots, now under the control of Overlord, converted others by injecting them with more nanobots, which replicated themselves and continued the process. There were one hundred test subjects in the group that received the plague cure. Almost overnight, there were a thousand cyborgs. And from there, you can imagine what happened."

"But," Oliver said, "it would have taken years for an A.I. to evolve like that. How did they not see it coming?"

"Because it did not take years. It took just under one second."

"One *second?*"

"That is a very long time for an A.I., as I understand it. Regardless of whether it was one second or two, this led to armed conflict between what were now called the cyborgs and everyone else. The American Federation was in a full scale war against the cyborgs within a day."

"But war doesn't make sense," Oliver said. "Didn't the cyborgs want to convert people, not kill them?"

"Certainly. They anticipated humanity would surrender, eventually. Killing was only a means to that end, a matter of simple calculation. Humans are easily replaceable, after all. You people breed like…well, humans."

"Gross," Jeffrey said.

"Eventually, a cure was developed. A code transmission. A patch, as Seven would say. It left the nanobots functional but disabled the Overlord program. The cyborgs were no longer under its control. War became peace in the time it took the patch to wrap its way around the globe. A few minutes, in other words."

"Why leave the nanobots functional at all?" Oliver asked. "It seems like they were nothing but trouble."

"By that time they had become so deeply integrated into their host bodies that shutting them down entirely would have killed the hosts, as well. I believe you saw the cyborg's armor. It was not worn by the cyborgs; it was grown. Their internal organs were converted as well, which made them very hard to kill. The nanobots were capable of repairing anything other than massive damage."

"Why doesn't this story have a happy ending?" Jeffrey asked. "It seems like there should have been hugs and kittens for everyone, at that point. Everyone likes hugs and kittens."

Artemis nodded. "Indeed. However, the scientist who developed the cure was killed in a cyborg attack at her research facility shortly after she transmitted it to Federation Command for analysis and deployment."

Oliver had a suspicion he knew where this was going. "It was someone close to Sally?"

"Her younger sister. Linnea Rain." Artemis smiled wistfully. "I liked her very much. She had a brilliant mind, but it was more than that. She was filled with such...*hope*. It was quite remarkable given what she had been through. She was a wonder."

"But Sally couldn't have just gone around shooting everyone," Oliver said. "Well, she'd probably *try*, but eventually someone would stop her."

"You are quite correct, Mr. Jones. During her research, Linnea also developed a virus that *could* disable the nanobots entirely. She only intended it to be used if everything else failed, but Sally found the code when she went through her sister's effects." Artemis took a sip of her tea. "In her grief and rage, Sally used her position at Federation Command to access the equipment she needed to transmit the virus. I begged her not to release it, but…I failed. The cyborgs were dead an hour later. All but one, it would appear."

Oliver took a moment to let that sink in. "My god," he said. "She really did kill them all."

"I always thought that was a figure of speech," Jeffrey said. "Like when someone says he's going to bring home a really big fish for dinner, but when he gets home the fish is just an average fish." He looked at Oliver pointedly.

"It was not just talk," Artemis said. "Afterward she was facing trial and almost certainly execution, especially given that she made no effort at all to hide what she had done. 'They had it coming' is not much of a defense, I'm afraid. I convinced Federation Command to let me bring her here, instead, with the caveat I guarantee she would never return. A life in exile would be better than death, I thought. In any case, that did not matter. When we arrived here, Sally smashed our mirror to pieces. She could not go home even if she wanted to."

Oliver nodded. He had no idea how he was supposed to react to all of this. "I guess I misjudged her," he said.

"How so?"

"She *is* a monster."

"No," Artemis said. "She is not. She made a mistake."

"I can't believe you're defending her," Oliver said. "It's…it's actually *genocide*, for god's sake. You call that a mistake?"

"I did not say the act itself was not monstrous. I would be careful who you call a monster, Mr. Jones. Should we ask the Kalatari what they think of you?"

"You did kill all those lizard people," Jeffrey nodded. "I was there. I saw it. You put the whammy on them."

"But I had no idea what I was doing!" Oliver protested. "And it's not like they were really people, anyway."

"They would have disagreed," Artemis said. "As do I. That was a rather callous statement, Mr. Jones."

Oliver already regretted having said it. He'd very nearly liked one of the Kalatari, even though he'd seen the man eat a human liver right in front of him. "Well, they *were* trying to kill me at the time."

"And if they had just murdered someone you loved, would you have been merciful to them?"

"But…" Oliver stammered. "The cyborgs had been cured. They were people again."

"True. I suppose it is a small mercy that they did not have very long to enjoy their restored humanity before she wiped them out."

Oliver could barely believe what he was hearing. Artemis could be cold at times; he assumed that was something that went along with her extended life span. He had never seen her just write off human life so easily, though.

"In any case," Artemis continued, "Sally serves me as a form of penance, if you will. Call it a work-release program. She is well aware she can never make up for what she did, but I will see that she spends the rest of her life trying. I can be satisfied with that."

"I'm not sure *I* can," Oliver said.

Artemis poured herself another cup of tea. "If you cannot, you are free to resign your position."

"*What?* Just like that?"

"It is simple math, Mr. Jones. She is worth more to me than you are. Even if she were not, I accepted responsibility for her when I brought her here. I cannot abandon that because it is inconvenient for you."

Oliver opened his mouth and then shut it again, not sure what to say next. "Would you really let me go?" he asked. "I remember when you offered me this job, you were ready to drug me and lock me up somewhere if I hadn't taken it."

"I was," Artemis admitted. "I was concerned your ability to alter reality made you too dangerous to leave you unsupervised. However, you have proven unable to do much of anything with your power since your encounter with the Kalatari. I like you well enough, Mr. Jones, and I believe you are an asset to my team, but I will not stop you if you wish to leave us. If you have any sense at all, however, you will at least take a few days to consider the matter most carefully."

Oliver wanted to pretend there was something to deliberate, but he knew there really wasn't. He had lived a very mundane life before he'd met Artemis and the others. Since then things had been anything but mundane. It was as if he'd spent his entire life watching a black-and-white television and one day suddenly switched to color. Things weren't always perfect in his new life, but he wasn't about to go back to a black-and-white one. "I'm fine," he said. "I was just shocked, I guess."

Artemis nodded. "That is fair. It was shocking news." She gave him a reproachful look. "It would have been much less shocking if you had read the files I provided you with earlier."

Jeffrey had been silent for a while. "You said it was a mirror?" he asked. Artemis nodded. "Does this mean there are different versions of us in Sally's world? Like, me and Oliver are there but we have little beards and we're evil?"

Oliver suppressed a groan. "No," Artemis said. "While there are many similarities between that world and ours, there are not copies of you there, much less *evil* copies. You are unique, little cat."

"Well, that's what I *thought*. I just wanted to make sure in case an evil me showed up and started causing trouble."

"I assure you that will not happen." Artemis sighed. "It occurs to me that I may have spoken too harshly to Sally earlier. To tell you the truth, Mr. Jones, I have not yet forgiven her for what she did. Perhaps I will someday. Perhaps not. I will caution you, though. If you cannot find it within yourself to be kind to her in the next few days, I do not want you near her at all. You may take sick leave with my blessing."

"We get sick leave?" Jeffrey asked.

"You do not technically work here," Artemis pointed out.

"Oh, yeah," Jeffrey said. "I'm more of a consultant."

"I don't…" Oliver started. "Never mind. I don't need sick leave. I doubt the subject is going to come up again."

"I am not sure," Artemis said. "Her reaction tonight was not what I expected."

"How so?"

"It was grief, Mr. Jones. She is…mourning."

"I think she's always mourning," Jeffrey pointed out. "She doesn't smile much."

"That is true, but I believe she is mourning her victims. I cannot recall seeing her do that before."

Oliver nodded. Sally usually bragged about having killed the cyborgs, but Oliver had never taken it very seriously. Of course, until tonight, he hadn't understood what that really meant. "So that's a good thing, right?"

"Perhaps so. However, Sally tends to be given to extremes. Given her course of action the last time she felt grief, I do not yet feel we should be celebrating."

But that had been a different case, Oliver thought. After her sister's death, Sally had gone after those she felt were responsible for it. But even if she *was* mourning the cyborgs, she was the one responsible for killing them. She could hardy take revenge on herself. And given that she could neither return home nor return the cyborgs to life, there wasn't much else left for her to do.

Oliver wondered why he wasn't more reassured by that thought.

Chapter 6

Oliver was back in the office at 9:15 the next morning. The first thing he noticed was the flowers. More than a dozen different arrangements littered Bruce's desk at reception. It looked like a florist's truck had crashed in their lobby. "What the hell?" he asked.

"We're popular this morning," Bruce shrugged. "I think it's about your trip to Romania." Artemis had recruited Bruce for the reception position from off of the street. Literally off of the street; Bruce had been panhandling for change at the corner of California and Drumm when she had found him. He was paid to be polite to visitors, intimidating on the rare occasions it was necessary, and for the fact he didn't mind sitting behind a desk full of weapons he wasn't afraid to use. He didn't speak much about his past, but Artemis had told Oliver once that the fact that Bruce had nothing left to lose made him ideal for the job. Oliver had no doubt Bruce would defend the office to the death, if necessary. He wasn't sure how much Bruce knew about their operations, but doubted he'd have been surprised if he'd been called into service to drag the dead cyborg into Seven's lab.

"Great," Oliver said. "It smells like…well, it actually smells pretty good in here." Oliver had wondered aloud before whether having a public office was such a great idea. He had imagined his team operating out of an abandoned factory, or a space station, or possibly the Batcave. When he'd found his new office was only a few blocks away from the hedge fund where he'd worked before, it had been a little bit difficult to hide his disappointment.

"Artemis wanted to see you first thing," Bruce said.

"Is she mad?"

"She's Artemis."

Oliver nodded. "Fair point." He wasn't sure he'd ever seen Artemis mad. Nor did he really want to. He started down the hallway.

Artemis was waiting behind her desk with a pot of tea when he arrived. She always seemed to have tea ready. Seven was already there, seated in another chair. "Come in," Artemis said. "The tea is hot. You should have some."

Oliver sat down and helped himself to a cup. "I saw the flowers," he said. "From the families of Dracula's victims, or something like that?"

"Not at all. They were sent by other vampires. Most of the major factions in the United States are represented there. I expect others will be forthcoming. It is still quite early in the day."

Oliver blinked. "Other vampires? They're…they're *thanking* us for killing one of them?"

"Dracula is a nuisance," Seven said. "Nobody can stand him."

"He makes it very difficult for the vampire community to remain inconspicuous," Artemis nodded. "A number of them clearly wished to express their gratitude. While I am unconcerned with their opinions, gratitude is always an advantageous thing." She nodded at Seven. "Fill Mr. Jones in, please."

Seven hadn't changed clothes and his hair seemed even more out of place than it had been the last time Oliver had seen him. He must have slept in the office, Oliver realized, if he'd slept at all. "As I thought, the poor bastard was on his last legs. The virus that got the others hit him as well but it didn't initialize properly, for reasons I don't understand yet. Rather than disable the nanobots entirely, it made them incapable of self-repair or replication. In time, they just started dying." He shrugged. "He was barely functional, to tell you the truth. He'd probably been in hiding all this time while he worked out how to get here."

"How *did* he get here?" Oliver asked.

"He had a teleportation device built into his armor. It looks like they finally got the technology working. Of course, he was the only one left who could use it."

"Can you reverse engineer it?" Artemis asked. "It could come in handy."

"Doubtful. It looks like it burned itself out during the trip, and Sally's guns did a number on what was left after that. If I had a year, maybe I could come up with something."

Oliver thought about it. "I'm not an expert, but when I

think of teleportation it's something going from place to place, not…"

"It wouldn't ordinarily work between worlds," Seven interrupted. "You're right. I have no idea how, but he must have found the American Federation's mirror and been able to analyze it. It was under guard the last I knew, but maybe they threw it in the trash or something. I'm surprised they didn't smash the thing."

"That does not answer how he got *here*," Artemis pointed out. "Our mirror *was* smashed."

"But the shards still exist. That may have been enough for him to get a general location. He only wound up 60 miles away from the vault. We'll probably never know for sure, though."

"In any case, remind me to have the rest of our mirror melted down," Artemis said. "I do hate destroying an artifact, but we have no further use for it, and it seems like it may be more trouble than it's worth."

The phone on Artemis's desk chimed and she pressed the intercom button. "Maria is here," Bruce's voice came over the speaker. "She has asked to see you personally. Are you available?"

Artemis considered it for a moment. "Show her back, please." She clicked the phone off. "This was inevitable."

Oliver was certain he knew that name, but couldn't place it at first. "Isn't she…"

"Yes, you've met," Artemis said. A moment later Maria appeared in the doorway and Oliver knew her immediately. She looked exactly as she had during their first and only meeting six months ago. Maria was Mexican and appeared to be in her mid-twenties, with dark hair and eyes as cold as her blood must be. She wore an immaculate brown suit with heels that made her about five-foot-six. In one hand she carried a small gift-wrapped box. She bowed to Artemis.

"My master sends you greetings," she said.

"How are you even…" Oliver began. "It's broad daylight outside. Why haven't you burned up?"

Maria smiled pleasantly at him and he caught the glint of her fangs. "I never went outside."

"Do you sunburn in your car, Mr. Jones?" Artemis asked. She looked at Maria. "I receive your master's greetings and send my own in reply."

Oliver nearly shook his head. He hadn't met a great number of vampires, but many of the ones he had tended toward formality. Maria took that several steps farther.

"My master thanks you for your recent kindness and prays you accept this small token," Maria said, proffering the box. Artemis nodded and Maria sat it down on the desk in front of her.

"Did you *all* hate Dracula?" Oliver asked as Artemis began to unwrap the box.

Maria glared at him. "He was a…" she hissed angrily before catching herself. "He was unworthy to be among us," she said, her voice calm again. "I begged my master for the honor of dispatching him myself, but he dislikes for me to leave his side for very long."

Oliver had met Maria's "master," as well. That was John Blackwell, a reclusive hedge fund billionaire who operated out of his estate in Sonoma, in the hilly wine country about an hour northeast of San Francisco. Blackwell was notorious for rarely leaving his property. Oliver had assumed he was just an eccentric until he'd actually met the man and discovered he also had fangs. As far as he knew, John Blackwell was the oldest vampire on the west coast, and certainly one of the most powerful.

"Oh, my," Artemis said. Oliver looked back to see her holding a small ivory figurine carved into the shape of a mouse. The figurine was astonishingly lifelike; the little mouse looked like it might scurry out of her hand and head for the door at any moment.

"That's cute," Oliver said.

"It's a *netsuke*," Artemis said, stroking the mouse with her index finger. She looked at Oliver. "Japanese. Mid-nineteenth century, I'd say. Mr. Blackwell knows I have a fondness for them." Maria nodded. "Please convey my appreciation of this kind gift to your master."

"My master apologizes that it is such a humble thing," Maria said.

"It is gratefully received."

"As you say, it will be done. I will now depart."

"Be well, Maria."

Maria turned and left the office. Seven looked at the *netsuke* curiously. "You want me to carbon date that?"

"Of course not," Artemis said. "It would be a crime to damage it." She placed the *netsuke* delicately on her desk and stroked its head.

"Is there a reason we fight some vampires and leave others

alone?" Oliver asked.

"Is it not obvious?" Artemis asked. Oliver waited until she looked at him as she might a small, stupid child. "Have you ever heard of vampires terrorizing Solano County?"

"Of course not. There would be a panic."

"Have you ever heard of a vampire terrorizing small villages in Romania?"

"Well, yes. That's why you sent us there."

"There is your answer. In any case, John Blackwell no doubt believes he owes me a favor now. *Another* favor, I should say. I spoke rather firmly to him after he failed to protect you at his estate."

Oliver nodded. Sally had taken him to hide out at Blackwell's house while the lizard people had been hunting him. One of the vampire's servants had bitten him in an attempt to turn him into a vampire and stage a coup against Blackwell. It hadn't ended well for her. Oliver's body had violently rejected vampire blood, and Maria had torn the servant's head off with her bare hands as punishment.

Maria reminded Oliver a little bit of an iceberg. On the surface, she looked harmless. It was what lay underneath that could tear you to bits. She was the only person Sally had ever shown the slightest bit of fear about dealing with.

"I guess you're right," Oliver said.

"I've been doing this for a very long time," Artemis said. "Of course I am right. How was your evening?"

"Fine, thanks." Artemis stared at him. "Oh, right, you don't make small talk. Nothing unusual happened. I watched TV with Jeffrey and went to bed."

Artemis nodded. "Very good. That is more or less what I expected. Have you spoken with Sally?"

"No. Is she going to be in today?"

"She will not. Tyler is keeping an eye on her."

Oliver hesitated, not sure about his next question. "How is she doing?"

"She is traumatized. That was to be expected. I believe last night was the first time she ever had to face what she did. I do not imagine it was easy for her. Frankly, I would send her on vacation, but she has nobody in her life other than us and I don't want her to be alone. In the past I felt that working was the best thing for her. I believe that remains the case."

"Yeah."

"Take the day to catch up on your reading, Mr. Jones. You will very likely need at least some of the information contained there in the future. Remember, information is our greatest weapon."

Oliver did exactly that. He intended to merely skim through the stack of files to make a good dent in it, but got caught up reading about a case dating back to 1932. A British submarine had sunk near Dorset, killing the entire crew. It took the British eight days to find it. Artemis's team had found it in three. Two of them had even gone down to the wreck to retrieve something identified only as "Package A-32." There was no mention in the file as to exactly what the package was or what it did, but it had been moved to the vault in southern Virginia shortly afterward.

The vaults fascinated Oliver. The Araneae Group had five

of them scattered around the world. Each was located deep underground in a fortified bunker. Each had only one access point protected by heavily-armed security personnel. The security officers couldn't actually reach the vaults they protected themselves; that was reserved for Artemis and her teams. Access required retinal scanning and voice print analysis. The vaults were the resting places of various artifacts and devices The Araneae Group had collected over the years. The things inside were either too dangerous to be exposed to the outside world, or they were things that needed to be protected *until* they were needed in the outside world. The nearest one was Vault 3, in Santa Clara, just an hour south of San Francisco. Tyler had gone down there on the day Oliver had accepted Artemis's offer to join the group in order to retrieve an item they needed for his first assignment. In hindsight, Oliver wished he'd gone along as well. He was curious what kind of wonders he might discover inside.

He'd find out sooner or later, most likely. Artemis ordered regular inspections of the vaults and their contents, and most of the company's files were kept in them as well. If Oliver got through the stack he was working through quickly, perhaps he could make an offer to run down to Santa Clara to pick up more in order to "further his education." And while he was down there, he could take a look around. Maybe he'd find the Ark of the Covenant sitting on a shelf. There were probably stranger things to be discovered there.

Oliver left the office just after 5:00 and took a crowded Muni train almost to its final stop, two blocks from his house. As unpleasantly crowded as the train could be, it was often faster than driving from one end of the city to the other at rush hour. By the time the train crossed 19th Avenue it was only about half full, making the rest of the ride a bit more pleasant.

Oliver considered making a stop to pick up some cheap take-out, but decided he might order a pizza when he got home instead.

The Sunset district was the only place in San Francisco Oliver had ever seriously considered living in. The hustle and bustle of the Marina or the Mission might appeal more to some, but the Sunset had a lazy residential feel that he liked. It was lined with small houses and had a wide variety of restaurants, and the nearest grocery store was close enough that getting there and back wasn't the hassle it would have been elsewhere in the city.

This was where he had met Jeffrey, who had been one of the neighborhood's many stray cats. He'd come to Oliver's windowsill one night to beg for scraps, although Jeffrey would have described it as "asking very politely" rather than begging. Oliver had given him some of his own dinner, and the cat had become a regular visitor after that. And then one night, in what was the first manifestation of Oliver's "power," he'd given Jeffrey the ability to speak. The cat had been so shocked by this development he'd immediately run away.

Oliver hadn't seen the cat again for some time. Eventually Jeffrey returned, demanding to be "put back" to the way he had been before. But on the same night Oliver had been attacked by the Kalatari, the lizard people who believed in a prophecy that Oliver would destroy them. Much to Oliver's surprise, that had proven to be exactly the case. By the time it was all over, Jeffrey had decided he liked being able to speak. Not that it would have mattered much if he hadn't. Oliver had never been able to control his power. It hadn't manifested again in any capacity since the night the Kalatari had met their fate.

In a way, he thought, he and Sally had that much in common. While he hadn't meant to destroy the Kalatari and would never even have known of their existence had they not shown up at his house, he did have to live with the guilt of what he had done. He could relate to what Sally must be feeling now, at least in some small measure.

Jeffrey wasn't in the house when Oliver got home. The cat still had a certain amount of wanderlust left over from his days roaming the streets, and Oliver typically left his kitchen window open in case he felt the need to get out and stretch his legs.

Oliver turned his television on to the local news and began rummaging through his kitchen cupboards. He had the ingredients to make a simple stir-fry, if he wanted to, but pizza still didn't sound bad. He wondered what Jeffrey would want. The cat insisted that he have dry food and water available at all times in the house, but still wanted some of what Oliver was eating most nights.

Oliver was checking the sell-by date on a package of chicken tenders when he heard a scampering at the windowsill behind him. "How was your day?" he asked, turning around. "You see any…" Oliver trailed off. As he'd expected, Jeffrey was sitting on the windowsill. Next to him sat another cat Oliver had never seen before.

"Meow," Jeffrey said.

"Oh," Oliver said. "Um…" He wasn't sure how to react. He'd never seen Jeffrey with another cat before. He hadn't even realized Jeffrey *knew* any other cats. Weren't male cats generally solitary animals, anyway? Then again, Jeffrey was hardly a normal cat anymore.

"Meow," Jeffrey said again.

Oliver hesitated "I was just…going to make some dinner, I think."

"Meow," Jeffrey said, nodding almost imperceptibly.

"I wonder what I should make," Oliver said. "I mean, that's what I'm asking myself right now, obviously, because I normally talk to myself in my own kitchen, and never to anyone else. I mean, unless they spoke English, and there's nobody else here who speaks English, I guess."

Jeffrey stared at him.

"I have some chicken in the refrigerator," Oliver said. "Maybe I'll fry it up with some bell peppers?"

"Meow," Jeffrey said, shaking his head ever so slightly. The other cat began washing its front legs with its tongue.

"I could order pizza?" Jeffrey appeared to be scowling at him now. "Chinese? Thai? Maybe Italian?" Jeffrey glanced at the freezer door, then back at Oliver. "I guess I'll check the freezer. Want to cover all my bases." He opened the freezer door. "Let's see. I've got frozen peas, frozen green beans, frozen corn, some of that tortellini soup I made last week. You liked that. I mean, *I* liked that. Frozen shrimp…"

"Meow," said Jeffrey.

"Okay." Oliver took the bag of shrimp and shut the freezer door. He looked at the bag thoughtfully. "Big problem with these shrimp is that they're frozen and it would take a few hours for them to thaw." Jeffrey glanced at one of the kitchen cabinets. "But there's a colander in there, of course." He took a plastic colander out of the cabinet and put it in the sink, then dumped the frozen shrimp into it. Running water would thaw the shrimp in a matter of minutes. "Well," Oliver said. "I guess I wonder if I want to eat the shrimp raw tonight." Jeffrey glared at him. "No, I'll definitely cook it. But now I can't remember what spices I like. I mean, I know *I* like spicy food, but not everybody does, and it's important I be considerate of my guests, even though I don't actually have any." Jeffrey nodded. "So I won't make it spicy. Maybe I'll just sauté it with a little bit of…lime?" Jeffrey shook his head. "Taco seasoning? Chili powder? Cumin and paprika?"

"Meow," said Jeffrey.

"Okay, cumin and paprika it is. I'll get right on that." Once the shrimp had thawed, Oliver peeled them and dried them with paper towels, then seasoned them with salt, pepper, cumin, and some mild paprika. Jeffrey watched the process intently, while the other cat began washing its forehead. Oliver put a sauté pan on the stove with a knob of butter and cooked the shrimp until they began to change color. He fished one out of the pan and tasted it. "Okay, that's pretty good, and by the way I'm never doing this again, so I really hope I enjoy this shrimp tonight, because it's the last time I cook shrimp for myself in my own house."

"Meow," Jeffrey said.

Oliver plated half a dozen of the shrimp and started for the windowsill, moving slowly so as not to startle the other cat. Jeffrey glared at him. "I…wonder what the problem is," Oliver said. "This shrimp looks and tastes perfect. It's delicious." Jeffrey considered that for a moment, then slowly put one paw out to his left and the other out to his right. He slowly looked from one to the other and back again.

"My hands aren't clean?" Oliver asked. "I'm not going to

eat with my hands." Jeffrey glared at him and looked back at the space between his paws, opening his mouth wide. "Oh," Oliver said. "Of course. These shrimp are much too big for me to eat comfortably." He took the plate back to the kitchen counter and began cutting them into small pieces. "Now I'll be able to eat these shrimp with no problem, and I'm also going to owe myself a huge favor for all the time I've taken to do this, so I better be damn sure I never pee anywhere I'm not supposed to *ever again…*"

"Meow," said Jeffrey.

Oliver returned to the windowsill and carefully placed the plate down between the two cats. "And now I guess I'll go in the other room," Oliver said. Jeffrey nodded at him as the other cat began to eat. Oliver went back to the pan, plated the rest of the shrimp for himself, and went into the living room to watch television.

Half an hour later he went back into the kitchen. The plate on the windowsill had been licked clean and both cats were gone. Oliver took the empty plate and put it in the sink. He'd deal with the dishes later. He couldn't help but wonder where Jeffrey and the other cat had gone. What did cats do on dates? *Was* that a date? Did cats even think in those terms?

He went back into the living room to find his cell phone buzzing, with Tyler's number on the display. "Hey," Oliver said.

"Hey. How was work?"

"There's nothing going on."

"Good. Did Seven find anything interesting with the cyborg?"

It occurred to Oliver how much his life had changed in the last few months. Was there anything interesting *besides* being attacked at their office by a cyborg from a parallel Earth right after they'd come back from killing Dracula? "Just that it was already dying by the time it got here. It had some kind of teleportation device it used, but we don't know much about that yet."

"They'd been working on that for a while," Tyler said. "Good thing the war was over before they got it working, or we'd all be screwed."

"Probably," Oliver said. It would have been difficult for anyone to fight an enemy that could disappear at will and reappear anywhere they wanted. "How's Sally doing?"

"She's been like a zombie, but she's coming out of it. Sally's a warrior. We'll be in the office tomorrow. I'd just as soon we had something to do to keep her busy and keep her mind off things."

They talked for a few more minutes, Oliver mentioning Jeffrey's "cat date," which Tyler found hilarious. "I can't believe you cooked them dinner," he said. "At this rate you're going to wind up with a litter of talking kittens."

"I'm not sure that's how it works," Oliver said. Then again, he didn't *know* that wasn't how it worked. He hoped not, anyway. One talking cat was already a handful. Half a dozen would be another matter entirely. "See you tomorrow."

"Good night."

Chapter 7

Sally and Tyler were indeed back in the office the next day. Sally looked a bit on the ragged side to Oliver's eyes, as if she'd been up all night and keeping herself going with far too much coffee. Oliver wondered whether she'd been unwilling or unable to sleep. He could well imagine her dreams were never pleasant ones.

On any typical morning when they were all in the city, the team would gather in the conference room for tea and their morning briefing. Artemis would advise them about any situations they were monitoring or give them new assignments. There was nothing urgent happening today, though, and the most interesting thing anyone had to talk about was Jeffrey's "date." Tyler brought up the idea of talking kittens again, which he still seemed to find enormously funny. "Could that actually happen?" Oliver asked Artemis. He'd have had to admit he'd been warming up to the idea, if only a bit.

"Unlikely," the girl replied. "He is biologically still a cat, after all."

"But his brain works differently now," Oliver pointed out. "He doesn't think like a cat. He thinks like a person."

"He can think any way he likes, but it does not alter what he is. If you began speaking Chinese, would your babies be Chinese?"

Oliver wasn't sure that was the best analogy in the world, but he was willing to let it go. Seven had perked up, though. "I can do a brain scan on him," he offered. "I'd love to map his neural pathways. Of course, I'd need another cat for a baseline, but I could probably work out how extensive…"

"That will do," Artemis said. Oliver doubted the cat would have been willing to sit still long enough for a brain scan, anyway, even if he wouldn't have considered it a gross invasion of his privacy.

"So you think he's not genetically different from other cats?" Tyler asked.

"Perhaps in some ways, but I would not think in any of the ones that matter." She looked at Oliver. "He can talk because you wanted him to talk. He can think because if he could not, he would have nothing to say. As you explained it to me, he was changed because you desired companionship. I doubt very much you were considering…" she paused. "There is no way to say that delicately."

"Just talking," Oliver said quickly. "Definitely not…anything else." While Oliver had been lonely at the time, he'd never been *that* lonely.

"Should we be gifted with talking kittens…" Artemis sighed. "Well, Mr. Jones, you must understand I couldn't have them, or at that point Jeffrey, running loose in the world."

Oliver nearly gasped. "You wouldn't *kill* them…" he began.

"No, certainly not. We have a place set aside for things that must be contained, in the event we can't control them."

"The island," Tyler said.

"We were going to send you there if you decided not to join us," Sally said. It had been the first time she'd spoken all morning. She looked at Artemis. "I'm pretty sure you almost sent me there once, too. Maybe you should have."

Artemis looked at her for a long moment. "And yet, I did not. You have value in this world, Salera. Do attempt to remember that, won't you?"

Sally took a sip of tea. "That's not my name anymore."

Artemis watched her for a moment longer and then looked away. "I think that's enough for this morning," she said. "Mr. Jones, you have files to review. I expect you to be a bit more up to speed the next time we talk. You are all dismissed."

Oliver spent the rest of the morning reading old case files. If he worked anywhere else he probably would have found file review boring, but at Araneae opening each new file was like starting a new science fiction novel. He could probably spend the rest of his life in one of the vaults reading and investigating the objects earlier lineups of Artemis's field teams had brought in. It wouldn't be a bad way to spend his retirement, if retirement was something the Group offered.

Did they have retirement? Oliver had never thought to ask before. Other than the ageless Artemis, nobody he had met working there was older than 40. Of course, if going up against lizard people and vampires was par for the course, maybe nobody lived much longer than that. Or maybe all of them eventually ran off to become priests in Cleveland, or conspiracy theorists, or…who knew what? Locked up in a mental ward didn't seem outside the scope of possibility.

Oliver joined Sally and Tyler for lunch at a Mexican restaurant down the street. A group lunch was a custom when they all happened to be in San Francisco at the same time. Seven joined them on rare occasions; Artemis never did. Whether that was a reminder that she was the boss or she just didn't care to eat at lunchtime, Oliver didn't know. He knew the girl *did* eat, having seen her do so, but it occurred to him that he didn't know if she actually *needed* to. That might be worth asking at some point, if he caught her in good enough a mood that she wasn't likely to take his head off for it. Artemis didn't suffer a lot of personal questions.

Sally only picked at her food as Oliver and Tyler ate. Oliver found himself wondering what he could say to make her feel better, but nothing came to mind. This wasn't the kind of thing Hallmark made a card for. The store didn't have a "sorry your past came back to haunt you" section next to birthday wishes and holiday greetings.

Oliver had been back in his office for an hour when there was a gentle knock at the door. He was a bit surprised to see Sally standing just outside. Normally she just walked in if she wanted to see him. "You got a minute?" she asked.

"Sure."

Sally took a seat in one of the chairs in front of his desk. That was another first; Oliver had never seen her sit there before. "I wanted to ask you something," she said, rubbing her hands together. Oliver waited. "It's about the lizards. The Kalatari."

"I think I know where this is going," Oliver said.

"You wiped them out. Your power…it destroyed their entire race."

"I know," Oliver said. "It's not something I'm proud of."

"Oh, I *knew* that. You felt terrible, I know. It's just…" Sally leaned forward slightly. "I remember you said once you didn't mean to kill them. You weren't trying to hurt anyone."

"I doubt I could have hurt them if that's what I'd been *trying* to do."

"Then how did you do it?"

Oliver didn't have a great answer. "You realize there's no Hogwarts for this, right?"

"I don't know what that means."

"Really? You've seen *Dracula* but you don't know *Harry Potter*?"

"I started with the classics."

"Fair enough," Oliver said. "I mean I didn't go to school for this. What I'm learning here, I'm learning from this," he held up one of the files, "but there isn't anyone like me. Everything in *my* file is stuff I already knew or put in there myself."

"But you did those things. You made Jeffrey talk. You wiped out the lizards."

"Yeah. With Jeffrey, I'm not really sure. I said things would be easier if he could talk, and suddenly he started talking. I didn't *will* for it to happen. I didn't wave my hands over him and say magic words. It just happened because on a subconscious level I wanted it to. I don't know if that makes much sense."

"It makes sense. What about with the lizards? You wanted them to leave you alone, so they all vanished?"

"No." Oliver thought about it. It wasn't that he'd wanted them gone, and it wasn't just because he'd wanted to live. It had gone deeper than that. "I didn't want to kill them, you understand? I wasn't trying to commit..." he stopped just short of using the word *genocide*. "I don't think I'm putting this very well."

"You've thought about bringing them back, haven't you?" Sally asked. "I know you must have."

"Is that what this is about? Bringing the cyborgs back?"

"Maybe."

Oliver nodded. He'd seen this question coming. "Yes. I have thought about bringing them back."

"But you don't. It's because you can't, isn't it? You would if you could; you're that kind of person. So what makes it different? Because it's easier to destroy than to create?" Oliver blinked. He'd heard Artemis use that line before more than once. He might also have seen it on *Star Trek*.

"No, because...you remember I'd been drugged more than once when all that was going on. I'd also been hit in the head quite a few times."

"One of them by me, I think. Sorry about that, by the way."

"It was actually the day before, but forget about it. I was barely aware of what was going on around me at that point. I thought I was delusional. I didn't believe the Kalatari were real.

I actually *said* that to the Matriarch just before…"

"Just before they weren't real anymore."

That was more or less it, Oliver thought. That, and the sound of rushing water that only he could hear that always seemed to accompany any manifestation of his power. It had been almost deafening when he destroyed the Kalatari. "Exactly. And the thing is, I can't just convince myself now that they *are* real and have them reappear. I know they're gone. I'd have to somehow trick myself into believing that they were up and walking around outside or something."

"You had to believe," Sally mused. "And what you believed became real. Interesting."

"I guess."

Sally stood up. "Thanks. Good talk. It was really…therapeutic for me."

"Oh," Oliver said. "Um…you're welcome." He watched as she left his office. That might have been the most unusual conversation he'd had in a while, he thought. It might have also been the longest he'd talked to Sally one-on-one before.

Jeffrey was waiting at Oliver's house when he got home later that night. "I was thinking we should have Thai food tonight," the cat said. "Something spicy with noodles."

Oliver had decided he wouldn't bring up the subject of talking kittens, but he was still curious about last night. "How was your date?"

"It was fine. She liked the shrimp, and she thinks you're very well-trained."

"She *said* that?"

"Not in so many words," the cat said. "We don't really have language. Well, not the way I do now."

"You're welcome, by the way."

"Oh," the cat said. "Thank you. I won't pee on your bed anymore."

"Thanks."

Later, over rice noodles that Oliver had cut into very tiny pieces so the cat could eat them without making a mess, Jeffrey said, "Do you think you could?"

"Could what?"

"Make her talk? Make her like me?"

Oliver sighed. Was this all anyone was going to ask him about anymore? "No. Not yet, anyway. Maybe someday."

"Oh."

"Would you really want me to?"

The cat thought it over as he toyed with a piece of chicken. "It would be nice to have someone like me around. It gets lonely, being unique."

Oliver nodded. "I guess that makes sense. Maybe someday, when I have some control over this thing I can do. I can't now. I'd probably just turn her into a clock or something?"

"A *clock*? Why would you turn her into a clock?"

"It was just an example."

"Oh. Okay. Do you want to watch *Star Trek* tonight? You've earned it."

"No."

They watched *Doctor Who* instead.

Chapter 8

A week went by during which nothing of any special note happened. There were no incidents involving ancient vampires, none with werewolves, and no aliens made their existence known. To be fair, Oliver had yet to meet an alien and wasn't entirely sure they really existed. Then again, he wouldn't have been at all shocked if during his reading he'd learned that Artemis and one of her previous teams had repelled an invasion from another galaxy at some point in the past. Very little took him entirely by surprise anymore.

Oliver finished going through the files he'd been assigned just before lunchtime and went into Artemis's office to report. He waited as she set a clothbound book she'd been reading aside and was surprised to see he recognized the title. "*The Other Side of the Sky?*" he asked. "That seems like an odd choice for you." He'd read the book as a teenager. It was the first in a series of fantasy novels about a man who traveled to a magical world and became a wizard.

"Why is that, Mr. Jones?"

"Because it's not an ancient text written in a language I can't understand. I didn't know you read for fun."

"I do, but today I am not. You are familiar with the book?"

"I read it a long time ago. It's kind of a Tolkien knockoff, if I remember it right. Elves and fairies and all that. Did you know the author disappeared? I think it was during the 1950's. He went for a walk one day and nobody ever saw him again."

"That may not be entirely correct," Artemis said. "However, it is not important at the moment. You have finished the files I gave you?"

"I did."

"Did you learn anything interesting?"

Oliver thought it over. *Everything* he had learned had been interesting, but he knew full well Artemis was going to want him to say something specific. "I was surprised the Loch Ness Monster was real." According to the file, it had died of old age in 1847.

"Ah, yes," Artemis nodded. "The poor, lonely creature. Last of its kind for all those years."

Oliver hadn't thought of it that way. The file hadn't referenced *other* Loch Ness Monsters, but logically, the creature had to have ancestors. "Yeah. I guess being unique really isn't easy."

"Are you referring to me, Mr. Jones?"

"No, I was thinking of Jeffrey, actually. He said it could be lonely. I guess the same thing is true for you, though."

"Is it?"

Oliver's eyes widened. "Oh, my god," he said. "Are there *more* of you?"

The corner of Artemis's mouth twitched up ever so slightly. "No, Mr. Jones. Not anymore, anyway. But that is an entirely different set of files."

"Really?"

"No. There are no files on me." She tilted her head slightly. "Well, that is not entirely true. There are certain texts in which one can find references to my existence. When I was younger and did not have the luxury of being anonymous, I had to keep a higher profile. There were certain tribes, long ago, that worshipped me as a living deity."

"Really?" Oliver asked. He hadn't heard *this* story before. "How did you convince them you were a god?"

"By the many miracles I performed."

"You can perform *miracles?*" Other than her apparent immortality, Artemis had never demonstrated any other kind of power.

"Behold." She studied Oliver's head carefully. "What is that, Mr. Jones, behind your ear?" She leaned forward, plucked a quarter from the space just behind Oliver's right ear, and then displayed it to him. "And that is only one of my many amazing powers."

"But that..." Oliver sputtered. "That's just sleight of hand! It's the oldest trick in the book!"

"Of course it is, Mr. Jones. But a long time ago, it was the newest trick in the book. Sleight of hand kept me safe for a very long while."

"Wow. I never even thought of that."

"If you have a hat, I have another miracle involving the production of rabbits."

"You're just messing with me now."

"Yes," Artemis nodded. "But I am pleased that you have been learning. As we have very little else to worry about at the moment, this is the perfect time to further your education." She pressed the intercom button on her phone. "Seven?"

Oliver heard a whirring noise and then a metallic crash over the speaker. "Here," Seven said a moment later.

"Does Mr. Jones have vault access yet?"

"He's in the system. He's cleared for the elevators and the turrets shouldn't see him as a hostile."

"Turrets?" Oliver asked.

"Thank you." Artemis clicked the phone off. "Go to Vault 3 in Santa Clara. Return the files you have finished reading to the file room there and select new ones to study. There are rather more than you would be able to read in one lifetime, so do not make your selection too ambitious. You should also examine some of the artifacts kept there and discover their purpose."

Oliver nodded. "You want me to play around with them and see what they do?"

Artemis shut her eyes and Oliver wondered if she was counting to ten before speaking again. "I certainly do not want you to *play around* with them, Mr. Jones. You will find that each item there has a catalog number. You may reference the numbers in our database in order to learn about their identity and purpose. I encourage you to study this information diligently, and for the sake of this entire planet, do not *play* with anything."

"Got it."

"Be certain that you are able to discuss some of these artifacts when you return."

"Will there be a test?"

"Yes."

"Oh." Oliver hadn't really been serious with that question, but he knew that Artemis was serious with the answer. "Okay, then. Um…I've never actually been to any of the vaults before."

"There is a first time for everything, is there not?"

"I mean, I don't know where it is."

"Ah, of course. Ask Tyler to drive you there. It would be unwise of you to enter without knowledge of our security protocols, in any case."

"I can take him," Sally said from the door. Oliver looked up in surprise. He hadn't heard her there. She shrugged. "I don't have anything going on and I'd like to get out for some fresh air, if that's all right."

Artemis nodded. "Good. I am pleased to see you taking initiative to help."

"I'm just getting some air, not saving the world," Sally said.

Artemis looked back at Oliver. "The vault is very large. I don't expect you to unlock all its mysteries in one afternoon, of course. That would be quite impossible. Take your time, and do be careful in there."

"Could anything in there kill me?"

"Death would be the least of your worries."

Oliver was beginning to reconsider his previous desire to get into the vault and start exploring. "I'll take good care of him," Sally said with a smile that was probably supposed to be reassuring, but had exactly the opposite effect. "Come on, Oliver. It'll be good for you to see what we've got down there. You never know when it's going to come in handy."

Chapter 9

There wasn't much traffic on the freeway and they made good time to Santa Clara in Sally's Miata. "You're going to love this," she said as they approached the city. Her obvious excitement was a nice change in her demeanor, Oliver thought. Getting out of the office obviously agreed with her.

Oliver, on the other hand, was no longer so sure this had been a good idea. Artemis had never explained exactly what she'd meant by "turrets," but there seemed to be only so many possibilities. None of them involved a welcoming committee with punch and cookies.

He would have had to admit to some surprise when Sally exited the freeway and turned into a gated retirement community with a large sign that read *Casa de Flores* out front. "You've got to be kidding me," Oliver said. "The vault is in here?"

"If you were looking for it, is this where you'd go?"

"Well, no."

"There you go, then." She pulled up to a small security booth next to the entry gate and handed her company ID to the guard inside. He took a look at it and then scanned it with a handheld device. Oliver heard a series of beeps, and then the guard handed the badge back to her. He looked at Oliver expectantly.

"Your ID," she said. Oliver gave Sally his identification badge and she handed it to the guard, who put it through the same procedure as before. Oliver heard the same series of beeps and the guard handed the ID back.

"You're good to go. This the new guy?" he asked Sally.

"Oliver Jones, meet Handsome Dan. Dan, this is Oliver."

"Hey," said Handsome Dan.

"Hey," said Oliver. Oliver thought Handsome Dan might have been more aptly called Average Dan, but he didn't feel the need to point that out.

"Have fun in there," Handsome Dan said. He hit a switch to open the gate and Sally drove through it, stopping the car on the other side and waiting for the gate to roll shut before moving on.

Casa de Flores looked to consist of about 40 small ranch-style houses laid out in a rectangular grid. The houses were identical, each with a single-car garage and painted tan with brown trim. It looked to Oliver more like a painting than a place people would choose to live. "It looks like they've got a pretty strict Homeowner's Association here," he said.

"We *are* the Homeowner's Association."

"Seriously? Araneae owns all these houses?"

"Every single one."

Oliver looked up and down the street as Sally drove. Plenty of older people were out and about in shorts and shirts that looked like they were last in style at around the time *Leave it to Beaver* had been popular. None of them appeared to have a care in the world. A few even waved as their car passed by. "Who are all these people, then?" Oliver asked. "They can't be your security force."

"No, of course not. Artemis found them. Most of them are older people who were having money problems and looking at spending the end of their lives alone and in poverty, or worse. They get a free place to live in return for not asking questions about the house we're heading for. Well, and for being the biggest bunch of busybodies on the planet. If these people see anything out of the ordinary, no matter how small it is, the phone in the security office goes nuts. That's exactly how Artemis wants it."

"Was that the security office we just passed? Handsome Dan? No offense, but he didn't seem like much."

"No, that's just the public face. The security office is…" Sally pointed at one of the houses. "That one. Those guys have enough firepower to put a SWAT team to shame." She pointed at another house across the street. "And that one isn't even a house; it's just a façade. The front part slides into the ground and there's an Abrams M1A1 in there. We've got another one on the next block."

"M1A1? That's…" Oliver thought about it. "That's a tank."

"Well, they're not just something we picked up at a military surplus sale. They're very good tanks. And just in case everything else goes to hell, the entire vault is lined with enough explosives to turn the whole thing into a crater. Artemis and Seven are the only ones that can detonate it, though."

"You're not serious?"

"Do I normally make jokes? There are five vaults now. Fifty years ago there were six. Some of our predecessors had a very bad day a while back. I don't know all the details. They had a dinosaur egg that hatched or something like that."

"Wow."

"I wouldn't bring it up to Artemis. She's still pretty pissed about it."

Oliver made a mental note to avoid that subject. He wondered if he'd be able to find the files relating to *that* incident today.

As they reached the last house on the street Sally entered a code on her phone and its garage door opened. She pulled the car inside and shut the door behind them. "Come on," she said, getting out.

A door led from the garage into a hallway, and from there into the living room. The house looked entirely typical in every way Oliver could think of. The furnishings were modern, if not particularly elegant. There were framed family photos on the walls of people Oliver had never seen before. A television and stereo system filled an entertainment center set in front of a long couch. Nobody seemed to be home, though. Oliver said as much to Sally.

"Nobody is ever home," she replied. "This one stays empty. Come on." She opened a set of white French doors that led into an empty closet. "This way."

Oliver poked his head into the closet. "There's nothing in here."

Sally put a hand on his back and gently pushed him inside. "Of course there isn't. You think we keep everything in the living room?" She joined him in the closet and pulled the doors shut. "Now hold still and keep your eyes open." She cleared her throat. "Identify."

Oliver heard a faint humming sound in the darkness that seemed to be coming from all around them. Then a thin rectangle of light appeared above their heads, lining the four walls of the closet. For the life of him, Oliver couldn't tell where the light was coming from unless it was being generated inside the walls themselves. The light dropped down to eye level, forcing him to squint just a bit, but he kept his eyes open. The light then dropped down to their feet, before slowly rising up the walls again.

"Nice," Sally said. "You didn't get electrocuted."

"Was that really a possibility?" Oliver asked.

"Well, you wouldn't have been electrocuted to *death*. Just a little bit."

Oliver heard a series of beeps. "Sally Rain," she said. "Alpha access." Another beep sounded. Sally looked at Oliver expectantly.

"Um…Oliver Jones." He looked at Sally questioningly. "Alpha access?"

The confirmation beep came and then the closet lit up, the light source still seeming to be the walls themselves. He heard a grinding as if heavy machinery was stirring into action, and then the entire closet began to descend.

"It's an elevator," Oliver said.

"No, it's a space ship. Of course it's an elevator."

The elevator closet lowered them for about five full minutes, leading Oliver to wonder exactly how deep they were going. It was very difficult to gauge the elevator's speed with no point of reference. Could it have been half a mile? How had the vault been created in the first place? It would have taken months to dig out, and how could that have been done without anyone knowing? Asking Artemis about it would probably be a waste of time. It was one more thing he'd have to check those files for. But then the elevator doors opened revealing the warehouse of Oliver's dreams, and he found he didn't care where it came from anymore.

Vault 3 was easily the size of half a dozen football fields, with a high ceiling lined with lighting fixtures from one end to the other. High shelves were arranged in parallel rows with wide aisles he could have driven a truck through. The whole place looked like a Costco, but instead of bulk-packaged household items, these shelves held a dizzying assortment of different objects. Some looked quite ordinary, while others looked like they might have been thousands of years old, and some looked like they might have originated on an alien planet. It was just as well that Artemis didn't expect him to study the vault in just one day. Cataloging this place could take weeks, or even longer.

"How many…" Oliver began.

"Who knows? I never spent much time here," Sally said. "And most of my first visit was spent hiding from the security system. That thing doesn't mess around."

Oliver looked at her. "This is where you came through?

From your world?"

"Come on, I'll show you." She led him down an aisle packed with what looked like Egyptian artifacts. Each item had a small plaque with an identification number next to it. "Those are for the database," Sally told him when he stopped to read one. "You can look them up in the computer room. Some of the newer stuff has a touchscreen display with it you can use to pull it up right there, but there's just way too much and we don't have a guy who maintains the place full-time. There was a guy years ago…"

"Don't tell me something in here killed him?"

"No. It was before my time. Artemis said he just vanished in here one day. Went walking down an aisle and never came back. She seems to think he'll show up again, eventually, but I don't see how. If you see anyone in here who isn't us, though, let me know."

Oliver couldn't tell if she was joking, but decided she probably wasn't. He resolved to keep his eyes open, and also to keep his hands to himself. He didn't want to wind up vanishing.

Sally turned a corner and stopped. The remains of what had once been a tall rectangular mirror with a wooden frame sat cordoned off with red tape that surrounded it in a circle. The frame had been bashed into several large pieces and shards of glass surrounded it. "There it is," she said.

"You came…*through* this?"

"Yeah. It's a gateway. Or, it *was* a gateway." She knelt down and took one of the shards in her hand. "It's just glass now." She held the shard up so he could get a better look.

Oliver could see part of his eye reflected in the piece of mirror. "How did it work?"

"You just walked through it and came out on the other side." Oliver took a hesitant step backward. "Don't worry," Sally smirked. "It only works if the mirror's intact. My team found ours in a bombed-out museum back home. We'd…" she paused, her eyes taking on a faraway look. "We were caught behind enemy lines and we'd been scavenging, trying to find anything we could use. At that point I'd have been happy with a few rusty old swords." She smiled ruefully. "There wasn't much in there, but when we found this mirror…"

"It brought you here."

"It did. To *this* place," she said, waving her hand at the shelves. "And this stuff was *exactly* what we needed. Except the minute we came through it tripped the security system and we got pinned down by the turrets. We couldn't even get back to the mirror to get away. We were stuck in here, hiding under shelves, until Artemis and her team showed up."

Oliver looked around. "I don't actually *see* any turrets."

"You don't *want* to see the turrets." Sally put the mirror shard back down on the ground where she'd found it. "Artemis wanted me to clean this up, but I'm a little attached to it. It's the last piece of home I have, even if it's only a reflection."

Oliver nodded. "You must really miss it."

"Sometimes," Sally said. "But it doesn't matter anymore. There's no putting this thing back together." She stood up. "The file room and the computers are over there," she said, pointing at a set of doors along one of the far walls. "Grab an armful of stuff to read back at the office. Then you should spend some time looking around and checking database entries. Artemis is going to expect you to be able to talk about some of the things you saw here. See if you can impress her."

"But there's so much in here…"

"You don't have to present a dissertation. Just if, I don't know, you had to fight an Arcadian wildebeest, you'd know you could come down here and grab a gamma tetradoxalyzer to handle it."

Oliver blinked. "Arcadian…"

Sally laughed. "I made all of that up," she said.

"So there are no Arcadian wildebeests or gamma…" he'd already forgotten the next word.

"I hope not. Then again, who knows? Take your time. I'm going to poke around a little, too. When you're done there's something I want to show you, if it's still here."

"What is it?"

"It's a surprise. You'll love it, trust me."

The file room alone turned out to be bigger than their entire office in San Francisco. Oliver spent fifteen minutes trying to figure out the cataloging system but completely failed to work out how the files were organized, so eventually he just grabbed an armful out of a cabinet at random. He'd have plenty of time to read them back at the office later. Files weren't what he'd really come here to see, anyway.

The vault's shelves were another matter entirely. Oliver spent a good two hours wandering up and down the aisles, examining different artifacts and taking note of their catalog numbers, and then using a computer to look up their entries. He didn't find the Ark of the Covenant, but the things he did see boggled his mind.

Sally finally appeared at the entrance to the computer room as he was reading. "Find anything interesting?"

"Did you know there's a knife in here that can cut *anything*?" Oliver asked.

"That could come in handy sometime. You should try to remember where it is."

"And there's a little statue of a dog that came out of an Egyptian tomb. It's related to the Spanish Flu that killed half the world in 1918 somehow but I'm still reading…"

"It killed half the world?"

"Well, no, but it was a lot."

"Come on, Oliver. I want to show you something. We're just lucky it's still here."

Oliver followed Sally down a series of aisles until they came to stand in front of what appeared to be an old submarine. It was about thirty feet long, large enough for a tall man to stand up inside, and shaped like a bullet with portholes spaced evenly down both sides of the hull. Rust appeared to have gotten the better of it at some point; there was no way this thing was seaworthy, if it ever had been. Oliver ran a hand along the smooth metal of its hull and knocked on it once with his fist. "What is it? I thought it was a submarine, but it doesn't have propellers. Some kind of bathyscaphe?"

Sally grinned. "You ready for this? It's a time machine."

Oliver pulled his hand away from the vehicle as if it were

about to catch fire. "Are you serious?"

"Absolutely," Sally said. "Can you believe it? This thing right here." She placed her palm on the vehicle's side. "It's an actual time machine."

Oliver wasn't sure what he would have expected a time machine to look like, other than a British police box or maybe a DeLorean. This device wasn't elegant in the least, but the thought of a real time machine right in front of him left him nearly speechless. "Wow."

"I know, right? I could hardly believe it, myself. Think about what you could do with it."

Oliver put his hand back on the machine. "Does it have a name?"

"Probably. I don't know. I just call it the time machine. It works for me."

"Where did it come from?" Oliver looked around for a plaque to find the identification number, but couldn't see one. "I want to look it up. The entry for this thing must be amazing."

Sally looked on the floor. "I didn't see it earlier. Maybe it got moved. Anyway, I don't know a lot. It was built during World War II by the Germans. They'd seen the end coming by that point and wanted a do-over."

"Holy *shit*."

"Yeah. I hardly believed that Nazi stuff when I was reading your history books. Anyway, Artemis sent a team to Berlin to steal it. She's pretty big on nobody being able to change the timeline."

Oliver walked in a slow circle around the time machine. It seemed to have no other features than the portholes and a hatch on the side one could use to gain entrance. "It's amazing. How does it work?"

"You'd have to ask a German physicist. Quantum something or other. Wouldn't it be amazing if we could use it?"

"It's not allowed?" Oliver asked.

"Oh, no," Sally shook her head at him as if he were a naughty child. "Artemis says it's too dangerous. But it's fun to know it's here. We could go anywhere. Or I guess *anywhen* might be a better way to say it. You could go back in time and see any historical event you wanted firsthand. Or go to the future and see how your life worked out. What would you do, Oliver?"

"I don't know," Oliver said. "Honestly, I never gave it any serious thought. Time travel is just a fantasy. Or it *was* just a fantasy. I never imagined it could actually work."

"You want to sit in it?"

"No," Oliver said. "I'd probably be too tempted to turn it on and see what it can do." He wasn't about to tell Sally, but seeing a time machine in person seemed like a good reason to catch up on *Doctor Who* tonight.

"Yeah, me too." She smiled at him. "What do you think it would be like to go back and see the dinosaurs up close?"

"I guess it would be amazing." Oliver imagined himself standing on a grassy hill, watching a Tyrannosaurus hunt in the distance. "You'd sure have to be careful, though, or you could get eaten. And you'd have to make sure you had enough gas, or whatever fuel it takes, so you could get back."

"Right. Wouldn't want it to be a one-way trip."

"No." He peered through one of the portholes, but it was too dark to see what was inside. "Was it ever used?"

"Sure. Operation Valkyrie worked the first time."

Oliver knew a bit of World War II history. "Hitler was actually *assassinated*?"

"Yeah. They blew his ass to hell. Then the Nazis went back and managed to change it. Seems like a waste of a time machine to me."

Oliver nodded. Most people thought about *killing* Hitler when they talked about having a time machine. He could think of lots of better things to do with one than save the man's life. Actually, *anything* sounded better than saving Hitler. "What happens if you go back in time and kill your grandfather?"

"I don't know. I'd try to avoid killing your grandfather if you ever take it out for a spin."

"What would *you* do?" Oliver asked.

"Hard to say," she shrugged. "A lot of your history is still pretty strange to me. Maybe I'd go back and see some of it for myself."

"Amazing. You could meet Gandhi, or John F. Kennedy, or…I guess anyone you wanted. You'd just have to remember to only be an observer."

"As long as you don't change the past, you're fine." Sally patted the time machine's hull. "The possibilities are pretty endless, if you think about it."

Oliver examined the floor around the time machine again. "I still don't see its catalog number." He wanted to check the database to find out more about the device, but the interface only took numbers. There was no place to type in "time machine."

"Don't worry about it. We should probably get going. Oh, and Oliver? I wouldn't mention this one to Artemis when she asks what you saw here. Time travel is one of those things she gets really uptight about. She might not let you come back here if she thought you were getting any ideas about it."

"I wouldn't dare," Oliver said. "You're probably right, though."

"Of course I'm right. I've known her longer than you. Anyway, you want to get some *pho* before we head back? I know a good spot near here."

As it turned out, Oliver did want to get *pho*. But even as he ate his noodles, he couldn't get the idea of time travel out of his head. It was going to be hard to get to sleep tonight without thinking about the things he could do now.

Chapter 10

Another slow week passed by. Artemis had no assignments for them and the world somehow went on without the team needing to save it. Oliver would have had to admit he was getting a bit bored. It wasn't as if he enjoyed having his life placed in mortal danger, but it was difficult to make the transition from fighting a famous vampire to hanging around the office without feeling a bit let down. He spent most of his time reading files, but even though the files were interesting, he felt himself wanting to get out and *do* something.

If there was a light at the end of the tunnel for him, it was that once he finished going through the files he'd picked up at the vault he could ask to go back there in the name of doing more "research." Admittedly, what he meant by research was just ogling the artifacts that he wasn't allowed to play with, but he figured he could spend weeks in the vault without seeing the same thing twice. Maybe he'd even find the guy who had gone missing in there. He must have some interesting stories to tell.

Tyler used the time to take Oliver and Sally on a tour of even more of his favorite lunchtime spots. Oliver never failed to be amazed by how much the man could eat with no apparent weight gain, typically ordering two entrees to start with and almost always needing seconds. He'd been meaning to ask more about werewolf metabolism, but Tyler had admitted he didn't know all that much, himself. "We don't have conventions," he'd said once. "I wish we did. I could finally get some questions answered."

Oliver found himself spending more time with Sally during the lull in activity than he ever had before, although it might have been more accurate to say *she* was spending more time with *him*. Every time he turned around she seemed to be there, asking about how his research was going, asking about his day, and whenever nobody else was around, returning to her favorite subject: the time machine. Where would he go? What would he do? Wouldn't it be fun? Under other circumstances Oliver might have found the constant barrage of questions annoying, but the subject of time travel was one he found endlessly fascinating. He'd even found himself starting to daydream about it. He'd open the hatch, get behind the controls, choose a time, and off he'd go.

Sally only mentioned the time machine when they were alone, though. Oliver found it a little strange she even kept it from Tyler, but she'd explained that Artemis preferred them not to talk about it at all, even amongst themselves. "It's our little secret, okay?"

"Works for me," Oliver had said. He wasn't about to claim he understood why Artemis wouldn't even tolerate *discussion*, but he wasn't about to risk being banned from visiting the vault when there was still so much to discover inside.

Oliver was on the couch watching television after work one night when the doorbell rang. He glanced at the clock. "It's a little late for salespeople," he said. "I wonder who it is."

"You don't really have any friends," Jeffrey noted. Oliver glared at him. "I didn't say you *shouldn't* have any friends," the cat explained. "You just don't have people over. I'm not complaining; it makes my life a lot easier. I don't want to have to sit here saying *meow* and licking my butt every time you have company."

"You still lick your butt," Oliver said, going to the door.

"*You* lick your butt!" Jeffrey declared.

Oliver was more than a little surprised to see Sally waiting on his doorstep. "You busy?" she asked. She held a paper grocery bag in one arm.

"I…no, not really. What's going on?"

Sally stepped past him into the house. "Nice place. I've never actually been inside before." She'd been outside just once, he remembered, helping Tyler rescue him from a Kalatari ambush. They'd fled the city shortly after and Oliver hadn't gone back to his own house for several days.

"Hey, crazytimes," Jeffrey said from the couch.

"Hey, dog food," Sally said. She walked over and scratched the cat behind the ears. Jeffrey stretched out and purred loudly.

Oliver closed the door behind her, still unsure what she was doing there. "Do you need something?"

"I brought you some stuff," she said. She took a large bottle of tequila out of the bag.

"Oh. Um…I don't really drink." This was an

95

unprecedented level of familiarity coming from Sally. For a brief moment he wondered if this was her way of hitting on him, but he dismissed that idea almost immediately. Sally wasn't one to beat around the bush; if she'd actually had any romantic interest in him, he wouldn't have to wonder about it.

"You don't think you can drink with me?" she asked. "Don't worry. I got some margarita mix to go with it. You like them blended or on the rocks?" She looked at him. "You're probably a blended guy, right?"

No, she definitely wasn't hitting on him. "On the rocks is fine," he said, just a bit defensively.

"That's what I like to hear. And I got movies." She reached into the bag and fished out two shrink-wrapped DVDs she'd probably picked up at the grocery store.

Jeffrey looked at the covers. "*Back to the Future* and *Star Trek IV*," the cat said. "Oh, I like that one. Chekov says he has to find the nuclear 'wessels.' It's funny because Chekov is stupid."

"No, Chekov has an *accent*," Oliver said. He looked at Sally, now even more confused. "Is movie night a thing we're doing now?"

"Why not? I didn't think you'd be doing anything." She looked around. "You're not, are you? Nobody else is here?"

"Just us."

"Then get us some glasses and let's do this."

Jeffrey insisted they watch *Star Trek IV* first. "San Francisco looked so crazy in olden times," the cat said.

"This movie isn't even 30 years old," Oliver said. "It's not exactly ancient history."

"It is when you're a cat," Jeffrey said. "They probably didn't even have litter that clumps."

"I honestly have no idea," Oliver said. "I don't think all that much has changed for the average cat, though."

Oliver felt himself getting tipsy by the time Sally started *Back to the Future*. "Some people need a car to travel through time," she said, leaning back on the couch. "We'd just need our machine."

"I'd go back to the time of the great cat ancestors," Jeffrey said. Oliver had told him all about his visit to the vault the night he'd come home from his trip there. "I'd bring them Friskies and they'd worship me as a god."

"What would you do with our time machine, Oliver?" Sally asked. "What would you *really* do?"

"I still don't know," Oliver said. "I might go to the future, just to see what happens. I guess I'd have to make a list." His vision blurred for a moment as he watched Marty McFly struggle to make it to school on time. "Wow," he said. "This tequila is *strong*."

"I brought you the good stuff," Sally said. "You feeling it?"

"I want to try some," Jeffrey said.

"This would knock you right out, little cat," Sally said. "You'd need to gain about a hundred pounds of body weight first."

"Aw," Jeffrey pouted.

Oliver had seen *Back to the Future* half a dozen times over the years, which was just as well tonight. In addition to his intermittent blurred vision, he was starting to feel dizzy. The tequila seemed to have no effect on Sally at all, though. She kept peppering him with questions about time travel. "Just think about it," she said. "*Think*, Oliver. We've got a working time machine. We can do anything we want with it."

Oliver rubbed his eyes. In the distance he heard a faint noise that sounded like rushing water. He looked toward the kitchen. Had one of them left a faucet going? "Do you hear that?"

"Hear what?" Jeffrey asked. "I know I can't hear this movie, because everyone keeps talking."

Oliver was sure he hadn't left a faucet on, but now the sound of the rushing water was growing louder. He recognized the sound now, though. It wasn't really water at all; it was the same sound he'd heard every time he'd used his power to change things. He'd heard it the night he'd given Jeffrey the power to speak, and again when he'd destroyed the Kalatari. He looked at his margarita, unable to remember if it was his third drink or his fourth, or maybe his sixth. "I think I've had too many of these."

"Is it water?" Sally asked. "Do you hear water?"

Oliver nodded, then frowned. He hadn't mentioned that noise to her before. "How did you know about that?"

"I read your file." She smiled at him, but now her smile didn't look friendly at all. She looked like a spider that had just spotted a particularly juicy-looking fly. "The time machine, Oliver." She put a hand on the side of his head to steady it, forcing him to look at her. "Think about the time machine."

The sound of rushing water grew yet louder. Oliver looked at his margarita glass again. "Did you drug me?" He was aware that his speech was slurred now, and his tongue felt like it had doubled in size.

"Of course not," Sally smiled. But her eyes said she was lying.

"You put the whammy on him!" Jeffrey cried.

"Just think about the time machine, Oliver. It's real. It's right there in the vault. It works. We can go back in time."

Oliver shut his eyes. "We can go back in time," he said sleepily. "We can go wherever we want." The sound of rushing water was loud enough now that his eardrums felt like they'd shatter. And then, like a switch turning off, it was quiet again.

Oliver sighed deeply. He was exhausted, for some reason. Too much tequila. He felt the world still spinning around him, and then he promptly passed out.

Chapter 11

Oliver woke up on his couch with his head feeling like someone had taken a hammer to his skull during the night. Jeffrey lay curled up next to him, sound asleep. On the television the DVD menu for *Back to the Future* played on an endless loop. It would probably keep repeating until the end of time, or at least until someone shut the power off.

Oliver's mouth felt dry and tasted as if he'd been chewing on a dirty sock. He squinted against the sunlight coming in through his living room windows. "What time is it?"

Jeffrey stirred on the couch, not opening his eyes. "It's too early for this," he said.

Oliver picked up the empty bottle of tequila and examined the label, as if doing that was going to answer his question. "How much of this did I *drink*?"

Jeffrey stretched out on the couch and sat up to start washing his face. "You can't hold your liquor at all," the cat said. "You passed out before Marty McFly even got to the school dance."

"What the hell was I doing?" Oliver's memory was failing him. He remembered drinking with Sally, but he hadn't realized he'd had so much.

"You kept going on about how you had a time machine. It got pretty annoying."

"Where's Sally?"

"She left right after you conked out. She said she had stuff to do, and thanks for the movies. And then she said you should fry up some sausage for my breakfast."

Oliver doubted very much that Sally had said that last part. He squinted at the wall clock. "At least I'm not late for work. I'm going to take a shower."

"I'm going back to sleep," Jeffrey said, lying back down. "Put some music on for me, will you? Maybe some smooth jazz."

"Really?"

"Of course not. My playlist." The cat had spent a great deal of time picking out his favorite songs to listen to while Oliver was at work. He'd insisted on having a remote control available so he could turn the stereo on and off whenever he wanted. His playlist was heavy on old Michael Jackson albums.

Oliver got cleaned up, took two aspirin, and caught the train for the financial district. He was still having trouble remembering everything that had happened the night before. Oliver hadn't been kidding when he'd said he didn't really drink; in hindsight, he probably shouldn't have started off with a pail of margaritas. It had felt like a pail, anyway. If he didn't know better he'd have thought Sally had slipped something into his glass. That really wasn't her style, though, and even if it had been what motive could she possibly have had? If she wanted him knocked out she could just have punched him in the head. She'd done it before, and Oliver wasn't too proud to admit that Sally could have wiped the floor with him using no more effort than he did swatting mosquitos.

Oliver bought a large black coffee at a shop across the street from his building and then caught the elevator up to the 41st floor. "Good morning, sunshine!" Bruce called as he passed the reception desk.

"Do I look that bad?" Oliver asked.

"You've sure looked better." Bruce nodded at the water cooler. "You're going to want some of that. Hydrate yourself."

"I've got coffee."

"You're going to need more than that."

Oliver retreated to his office. He was beginning to wish he'd brought the bottle of aspirin along from home. He could always make a run to the drug store for more, if need be. There were only about six different Walgreen's within walking distance of the office.

The first earthquake hit about half an hour later. At first Oliver thought it was just in his head, but after fifteen seconds he realized the entire building was swaying, not just his own body. It was far from the largest earthquake he'd ever felt in San Francisco, but at that moment he'd have greatly preferred the ground to stay where it was supposed to. His stomach felt like it might decide to empty its contents into a trash can at any given moment.

Tyler passed by the door to his office a minute after the

earthquake had ended. "That was a good one, huh? What do you think? A five?"

Oliver would have said the earthquake felt more like a 14, but he knew the scale didn't go that high. "Yeah."

Tyler took a good look at him. "Long night, buddy?"

"There's a reason I don't drink. I guess I needed a reminder."

Tyler laughed. "You seen Sally? She's not in yet."

"Not since last night."

Tyler's eyes widened. "Holy shit, really? *You two*? Wow. I can't say I never saw you guys getting together, but I didn't think it'd actually happen..."

"Not like that," Oliver snapped. Then what Tyler had just said registered in the part of his brain that was still capable of processing language. "Wait, *what*? Me and Sally?"

"Why not?" Seven suddenly brushed past Tyler, making a beeline for Artemis's office. Tyler watched him go, then turned back to Oliver. "Well? Why not?"

"I don't..." Oliver stammered. "It never even occurred to me."

"Not even once? You guys are friends. She's beautiful. You're...kinda funny. Neither of you is seeing anyone. You get my point here?"

"I don't know if we're actually friends," Oliver said. "I think she tolerates me. And even if there was more to it than that..."

Seven rushed past Tyler again, this time heading for his lab.

Tyler watched curiously. "What's gotten into him?"

"Who knows what ever gets into him?"

"Fair point. Anyway, even if there was more to it than that?"

"Well, we work together, for one thing. I can't imagine it would be a good idea. Besides, she's…"

"What?" Tyler asked. "Not your type?"

"It's not that. It's more that…she's absolutely terrifying."

"You never struck me as someone who has a problem with strong women."

"Strong women, no, but Sally's like the Godzilla of women."

Tyler shrugged. "She's pretty fierce, I'll give you that. I think you'd be a cute couple, though. You'd analyze things, she'd break them."

"I think you're totally insane."

Tyler smirked. "You up for lunch today? Something nice and greasy?"

Oliver's stomach flip-flopped. "Oh, you bastard." Food was the last thing he wanted to think about right now. Greasy food, even less.

"Sorry. I couldn't help it. You want an aspirin? There's a first-aid kit in the…" Seven rushed past again, this time nearly bowling Tyler over. "Hey!"

Oliver felt his stomach starting to sway again. A moment later he realized it wasn't his stomach; it was everything else. "Another earthquake?" he asked. Their building was moving again, and looking through his window he could see several other skyscrapers were, as well. There also appeared to be some kind of shimmer in the air, like he might see when there was a gas leak, but that could have just been his eyes rebelling against the sunlight.

"Maybe it's the big one," Tyler said, putting his hand on the wall. "Are we supposed to get under the desks or something?"

"If this building goes down I don't think being under a desk is going to help that much."

Oliver's phone chimed and Artemis's voice came over the intercom. "My office. Now!"

"You want me too, boss?" Tyler asked.

"I want everyone. Have you seen Sally? She's not responding."

"Not yet," Tyler said. "We'll be right there."

Oliver and Tyler headed for Artemis's office. Seven was already there, tablet in hand. The building hadn't stopped swaying yet. In fact, it seemed to be getting worse. "Should we be evacuating?" Oliver asked.

"Or getting under our desks?" Tyler chimed in.

"It doesn't matter," Artemis said, studying the readout on Seven's tablet. "This isn't an earthquake."

Oliver blinked. "It's not? Then what the hell is it? Did a bomb go off?"

"It's a timequake," Seven said.

"What the hell is a…" Oliver began.

"It's like an earthquake, but with time," Seven said.

"Oh. Of course it is." Oliver looked at Tyler. "Do you know what that means? I kinda need the simple version."

"That *was* the simple version," Seven said. "We're in a hurry, so I chose easy words you'd be able to understand."

"I don't think it worked," Tyler said. "I don't know what it means, either."

"Oh for god's sake," Seven said. "A timequake is…"

"There," Artemis said, tapping the tablet screen. "That's the epicenter. It's coming from Vault 3."

"How?" Seven asked. "Nobody could have gotten in there. Turrets are online but dormant, no security alerts. It's green across the board."

Oliver looked through Artemis's window. "Um…guys? You should probably take a look at this."

Artemis's window faced the Embarcadero where an outdoor park adjacent to the waterfront was often used for a farmer's market. Oliver liked to pick up fresh vegetables to take home after work, and for the ever-hungry Tyler it was like an open-air candy store. Today it looked a bit different, though. Twelve cyborgs could be seen marching up Market Street, outfitted in metallic armor similar to that of the cyborg that had attacked them in the parking garage. Each appeared to have a weapon held at the ready, although from this distance it was hard to tell exactly what they were. Oddly, only about half the people on the streets outside seemed to be able to see them. Those were moving out of the way, while everyone else went about their business as if nothing were out of the ordinary. Admittedly, one did develop a tendency to ignore the unusual after a few weeks of living in San Francisco, but this was going beyond the pale.

"We're under *attack*?" Tyler asked. "How is that even possible?"

"The attack already happened," Artemis said. "Reality is being rewritten around it. We're just catching up to it now." She turned to Seven. "How far back?"

Seven studied his tablet, sweeping his fingers over it and pressing the touchpad almost more quickly than Oliver could see. "Fourteen months, give or take. A little more time and I could pinpoint it, but time is something we're out of."

"How?" Tyler asked. "How is this happening?"

"Vault 3?" Oliver asked. "You said that's the, what, the epicenter?"

Outside the skyscraper at One Market Street shimmered and then disappeared into thin air. "Jesus!" Tyler screamed.

"Never mind," Artemis said. "It wasn't there anymore. It hasn't been there for a long time. What about Vault 3, Oliver?"

"Well, if it's a timequake, doesn't it make sense that it would have something to do with the time machine? That seems kind of obvious to me."

Artemis stared at him. "What do you know about the time machine?"

"Sally showed it to me. She said we weren't allowed to use it because of changing the past and all that."

"Oh, god," Seven said. "She could not possibly have been that stupid."

"We have a time machine?" Tyler asked. "Why am I just

hearing about this now?"

"Mr. Jones, this is very important," Artemis said. "Did Sally tell you the time machine was in working order?"

"Of course," Oliver said. "What would be the point of a time machine that didn't work?" He looked around. "Where *is* Sally, anyway?"

"No doubt in Vault 3. Or she was. Where she is *now* I could only imagine, but given the events outside, I strongly doubt she survived her attempt." She sighed deeply. "Damn her. No, damn *me*. I should have seen this coming."

"Can someone tell me what's going on?" Tyler asked.

Artemis pointed at Oliver. "She knew you could change things, Mr. Jones. If you believed something strongly enough, you could make it real."

"Believed what?"

"The time machine hasn't worked since 1945," Seven said. "The quantum drive was destroyed and even if we wanted to fix it, we don't have the materials to make a new one."

The pieces were beginning to fit into place now. "She told me it worked," Oliver said. "It was all she could talk about the last week. It was all I could even think about. Then she came over last night and…I think she might have drugged me."

"No," Tyler said.

"Just enough to get my mind wandering like it had…" he looked at Artemis. "I heard the water. Like when I made Jeffrey talk, and when I wiped out the Kalatari. It was the same noise I heard those times."

"You changed reality," Artemis nodded. "You believed the

time machine worked, and so now it does work. And Sally turned it on."

"She went back fourteen months," Seven said. "Before the mirror was broken. Before the war ended. She went home."

Oliver looked out the window. More buildings along the Embarcadero had vanished, and new ones of a different design had appeared in their places. They were tall, silvery metal structures, with pulsating blue lines running from base to tip. Oliver had never seen construction like that before. Well, he had, but only in science fiction movies. It looked like the cityscape of an alien metropolis in a distant galaxy.

"She tried to change what she did," Tyler said. "Well, of course she did. She didn't want to be a murderer anymore." He sighed. "God damn it, Sally."

"That much she succeeded at," Artemis said. "The cyborgs were not destroyed. Unfortunately, it appears that the cure was not deployed, either. There can be little doubt they conquered their own world and then invaded ours. They would have discovered the mirror, of course. It appears they did not meet with much resistance."

"What do we do?" Oliver asked.

"Nothing," Artemis said. "It has already happened. This timeline will be gone in a few more moments and we will find ourselves in a new one. You won't remember ever meeting me, Mr. Jones."

"What about us?" Tyler asked. "Me and Seven?"

"Difficult to say. I would have been aware of the fracture shortly after it happened and activated our emergency protocol for this kind of situation."

"The house on Filbert Street," Tyler nodded. "Can it correct the timeline?"

"No," Seven said, "but it will correct *us*. From there we'll work out a plan. But you and I won't know what's happened. Only Artemis will. If we're not with her we'll have no idea…"

"Do not fear," Artemis said. "I will find you." She looked around the room. "I will find all of you. I promise."

The walls of the office shimmered and Oliver suddenly found he could see through them. "But what about you? Won't you change, too?"

Artemis smiled wistfully at him. "I never change, Mr. Jones."

The office shimmered again, and then it was gone. For an instant Oliver found himself suspended in midair, then the world around him went black, and everything was gone.

Chapter 12

Oliver Jones had spent many idle moments at work daydreaming about what it would be like if he had a more interesting life. Stock analysis at the small hedge fund where he worked paid the bills, and he was quite good at it, but there was nothing particularly glamorous about studying Excel spreadsheets and crunching percentages all day. Not that Oliver needed glamour. Just a little adventure, once in a while. Some excitement. Certainly that shouldn't have been too much to ask.

He couldn't help but think the cyborg invasion of Earth was really overdoing it.

The first of them had arrived in San Francisco just over six months ago. Two hundred cyborgs had marched through a portal in Haight-Ashbury and begun "conversions" almost immediately. The conversion process consisted of injecting nanobots into a victim's bloodstream, where they began to replicate themselves. In short order they took over their host's higher brain functions. Oliver had seen the process more times than he cared to count. It looked agonizing, with the victims writhing on the ground as if their bodies were being controlled by a demented puppeteer. The screaming never lasted more than an hour or so, which was roughly how long the initial stages of conversion took. After that, cyborgs no longer expressed pain. Nor did they express any emotions at all.

The later stages, in which they would grow armor and one of their eyes began to glow blue, could take several days. Oliver was sure the internal organs were modified as well, in ways he didn't want to imagine. It was something he preferred not to think about.

Oliver considered himself something of an expert on the process. He was, to the best of his knowledge, the only human alive it had never worked on.

The cyborgs had taken San Francisco's financial district on the second day of the invasion. Oliver and his coworkers had spent the night hiding out in their office, waiting for the National Guard, or the army, or *anyone* to come and get them out of there. The cyborgs had come to their building instead, moving floor by floor, converting everyone they could find. Oliver had been huddled in a closet when they dragged him out, injected nanobots into his neck, and dropped him to the floor to undergo the conversion process alongside the rest of his screaming, writhing coworkers. But Oliver hadn't screamed. The injection had been painful, and he'd felt a hot flash afterward, but then nothing. When his converted former coworkers stood up and headed for the building's stairs to join their new comrades in their work, Oliver had just sat there staring at them. Eventually another cyborg passed by and injected him again, but exactly the same thing happened as before. There was a brief moment of heat, as if he'd developed a sudden fever, and then it was gone. After a third injection failed two baffled cyborgs had lifted him up and carried him downstairs, where he was quickly transported to a medical center near the Presidio for study.

Three months later the cyborgs had conquered most of the western United States, which was when they ran into a wall in the form of nearly every country on Earth with a military. If one good thing had come out of the cyborg invasion, Oliver thought, it was that nearly every other war being fought on the planet came to a quick end. Religious divisions and disputes over territory and resources became irrelevant when faced with a threat on this new scale. It was, in one sense, a great day for humanity. On the other hand, millions were either dead or had been converted, and there was no end in sight. The cyborgs had been unable to advance past the Mississippi river, and the nanobot-filled cruise missiles they fired east had been unable to provide them with any headway. The cyborgs believed that their teleportation technology would eventually turn the tide. It was what had gotten them to San Francisco in the first place, but where they had apparently found moving world-to-world easy, point-to-point travel had been for whatever reason much more difficult to master.

Oliver knew all of this because the cyborg scientists that had been studying him since his capture had been happy to tell him about it. They saw no reason not to. He was under constant watch in case he tried to escape, and even if he did, he had nowhere to go. The last human running around San Francisco wouldn't go undetected for very long, and the nearest human resistance group with any teeth operated out of the hills of San Diego County, eight hours to the south by freeway. Even if Oliver managed to steal a car, he doubted he'd make it a tenth of the way there.

Oliver had long since lost count of how many times he'd been injected with nanobots. The cyborg scientists had studied the results and determined that, through a process they couldn't understand, Oliver's blood reacted to the injections by heating up and burning the tiny machines to cinders. How this was possible without his superheated blood turning Oliver himself into a pillar of fire was a mystery. He never felt anything other than uncomfortably warm for a few moments, and once his blood was purged of the machine invaders it returned to normal.

The tests continued, however. The cyborgs seemed to have no end to the experiments they wanted to run on him. This was advantageous to Oliver only in that it meant they wanted to keep him alive and healthy. He was fed the same nutrient paste the cyborgs ate, which tasted foul but was surprisingly filling, was allowed to exercise in a fenced-off area outside, and was even provided with a television and DVDs to watch in his room. Armed guards were never more than a few feet away, but it beat the alternative. Oliver imagined they'd find a way to convert him one day, and then a machine would take over his brain and he wouldn't care anymore. He wasn't particularly looking forward to it.

Oliver was watching a British comedy show about a hapless secret agent when one of the cyborg scientists entered his room, syringe in hand. Two guards accompanied him, as was the usual. "Oliver Jones, we require a blood sample."

Oliver nodded. This scientist's designation number was SCI-3422XB. Each of the cyborgs had a designation that identified their function and other information to other cyborgs, although Oliver didn't know what all of the other information meant. He'd picked up that SCI meant scientist and SOL meant soldier, but that was about it.

SCI-3422XB wore a white lab coat over his armor, which made him look more than a little ridiculous. Oliver had asked about it once, given that there was no logical reason the cyborg needed to wear it, and SCI-3422XB had told him that it was intended to make Oliver feel more at ease with him. It came closer to making Oliver laugh, but he wasn't going to complain. If they really wanted to make him feel at ease, though, they could start by getting rid of the armed guards outside of his room.

"I'm not going to have any blood left one of these days," Oliver said, pushing up the sleeve on his blue hospital gown.

"That will not be a problem," the cyborg said. "We feed and hydrate you so that you will continue to produce more." He plunged the syringe into Oliver's arm. Oliver had stopped wincing at the less-than-gentle contact months ago. Being poked and prodded was so old hat now he hardly noticed anymore.

The cyborg filled two vials with Oliver's blood and withdrew the syringe. "Satisfied?" Oliver asked.

"For now. We have an interesting new set of tests to run."

"Oh?"

SCI-3422XB nearly looked pleased with himself, although Oliver knew cyborgs never felt pleased, or felt anything at all. "We have discovered someone else who cannot be converted. We intend to compare your blood to hers."

"Seriously?" Oliver asked. "Who is she?"

"A prisoner we captured nearby. It is a most unusual situation. She claims to be a vampire."

Oliver nearly laughed. He was about to tell the cyborg that vampires weren't real, but then again, it wouldn't have been very long ago that he'd have said that cyborgs weren't real, either. He wasn't sure if he was comfortable making any assumptions. "Well…that's pretty interesting."

"Indeed. We were unfamiliar with the concept, but we confirmed that she is averse to sunlight and must consume human blood to survive. She does not find our blood agreeable, so we intend to introduce you very soon."

"Oh?" That sounded ominous. "Should I be worried?"

"I suppose it depends," the cyborg said.

"On what?"

"On how delicious you are."

The introduction the cyborg had spoken of came the very next day. Oliver was led under guard into an empty operating theater and left alone. He spent a moment looking at himself in a large mirror set in one of the walls. It was probably one-way glass, he thought. Most likely all of the cyborg scientists were in an adjacent room, watching and waiting to see what would happen next.

After a few minutes the door he had been brought through opened again and two cyborg guards forced a woman in a blue hospital gown inside. The woman's hands had been bound behind her back with metal cuffs and chains fastened her arms to her sides. She hissed malevolently at the guards as they propelled her toward Oliver and then retreated through the door. The door shut, locked, and Oliver found himself alone with the vampire.

She didn't look like much, at first glance. The woman was

Mexican, with dark hair and eyes that lingered on Oliver for just a moment before scanning the room. Looking for an escape, Oliver imagined. Maybe she'd find a way out and leave him alone.

That was not to be. After a moment the woman turned her gaze back to Oliver. "What time is it?" she asked.

"What?"

"What time is it?"

"There isn't a clock in my room," Oliver said. "It's daytime."

"Is the sun out?"

"Ah…yes."

The woman grinned at him and he saw fangs glistening where her canine teeth should have been. "Well then, you understand I have to make this look good. And the truth is, I'm *very* hungry."

Now it was Oliver who wanted very much to escape, but there was no way out, unless he thought he could jump through the mirror into the observation room. The vampire took a step toward him. Even with her hands and arms bound, Oliver didn't think he had much chance of beating her in a fight, and he had just enough pride left that he wasn't going to start screaming and running around the room.

"We haven't met," he said. "I'm Oliver. What's your name?" Maybe if they made friends, she'd be less likely to eat him?

The vampire stared into his eyes for a moment. "You really have no idea, do you?"

"No. I've never actually met a vampire."

"You're wrong," she said. Then she moved at him so quickly Oliver's eyes hadn't even registered it until her fangs sank into his neck. Pain like fiery needles ran from the twin punctures all the way down his arm and he nearly screamed.

The vampire took several gulps of his blood and then released him. "You taste strange," she said, her breath cool on his neck. She looked at him quizzically. "You're not exactly human, are you?"

"I was the last time I checked," Oliver said. His knees threatened to buckle at any moment, but the pain from the vampire's bite was already receding, replaced with a dull throbbing that wasn't much worse than a mild headache.

"And you're already healing," she said, watching the skin of his neck. "Impressive. Chantal said there was something supernatural about you, but I suspected she was willing to say anything to keep me from ripping her head from her neck." She smirked. "She failed."

Oliver wondered if blood loss was making him delirious as well as dizzy. "What…the hell…are you talking about?"

The vampire shrugged as much as she was able to with her arms chained into place. "It doesn't matter right now. My name is Maria, by the way. You'll see me again." She turned to the mirror. "What else have you got?"

Two guards half-carried, half-dragged Oliver back to his room. When they had him situated in his bed SCI-3422XB put a needle in his arm and started an IV. "We must get your fluids back up, Oliver Jones."

"What did you really think you'd learn from that?" Oliver

asked. He was no longer in pain, but found himself oddly tired.

"To see if you'd live, firstly. To see if your blood can sustain her better than ours. At this moment we are examining her to see how your blood affects her system. Depending on the outcome, we may next want to see how her blood affects yours."

"You want to give me *her* blood?"

"According to the mythology we have accessed, that is typically how one becomes a vampire," the cyborg said. "If she is able to convert you, we will have learned something. If not, we will also have learned something. Life is full of mysteries, is it not, Oliver Jones?"

Oliver would have been inclined to agree, but at the moment all he wanted to do was shut his eyes and go to sleep. A moment later he did just that.

Chapter 13

Oliver woke up to find SCI-3422XB sticking another syringe in his arm. He watched as more of his blood was sucked into a tube. "You guys never stop, do you?"

"We do not," the cyborg said. "Unlike you, we no longer require sleep in the conventional sense."

"How long was I out?"

"All night, and most of the day. You seemed to need the sleep, so we did not wake you."

Oliver nodded. "Do you rest at all?"

"It is more of a recharging period," the cyborg noted. "You will find it very efficient, once we are able to convert you."

"Lucky me."

Oliver sat up in the bed once the cyborg had finished taking his blood. "How did your tests go?" he asked.

"It was interesting. Your blood had an unusual effect on the vampire. She appeared to be intoxicated for several hours after ingesting it."

"Really?"

The cyborg gave him a stern look. "Oliver Jones, have you been entirely honest with us?"

Oliver frowned. "About what?"

"The vampire was unusually talkative during her intoxicated state. In between threats to tear the heads from our bodies, she indicated that the two of you have met before."

"Really?"

"We can only conclude that one of you is lying, but we have been unable to identify what motive either of you might have for this."

Oliver shrugged. "I think I'd remember if I'd met a vampire before. Honestly, I thought they were just stories to entertain teenagers until I actually saw her."

SCI-3422XB studied his face for a moment. "You do not appear to be deceiving me. Then again, neither did she. This is a very strange situation."

Oliver tried not to laugh. *Everything* about the last six months had been strange. "I guess so."

"Further, the vampire indicated that her condition after drinking your blood was not the result she had expected. She suspects you are not really a human."

Oliver looked at his arm and brushed off a drop of blood that had formed there after the cyborg had removed the syringe. "You've done enough tests on me. Wouldn't you know if that was true?"

"We would expect so, but nor should an ordinary human be able to resist the nanobots. We initially suspected a genetic mutation, but that cannot explain the thermal reaction that takes place."

"Life is weird," Oliver said. "So now what?"

"Now we will see what effect the vampire's blood has on you. We will compare this to the effect yours had on her."

Oliver didn't see any more syringes waiting. "You're going to shoot me up with something?"

"No. We intend for you to drink her blood. Your mythology indicates this is the normal procedure."

"You understand how strange the word *normal* sounds right now?"

"Perhaps to you. We find new situations easy to adapt to."

"We're going to do this right now?"

"No, we must wait until dusk. The vampire has informed us that the change cannot take place during daylight hours."

Oliver had never heard of that before in any vampire story he'd ever read. "That seems strange."

"Indeed. We were unable to confirm this in any of the mythology we have studied, but nor could we confirm that it is false. A few hours should make no difference, and then we will discover the truth of the matter. Until then, perhaps you would like to rest and watch a DVD?"

Oliver didn't think watching old movies was going to make him feel any better about what was coming. "I'd like to take a walk, if you don't mind. It might be my last one."

"As you wish. The guards will convey you to the yard."

The cyborg left the room and shortly afterward two armed guards marched Oliver to the fenced-in area outside, where they watched as he walked along the yard's perimeter several times. Oliver found he wished he could see the ocean from where he was. It would have been nice to sit by the water for a while. If he really did turn into a vampire, he wasn't going to be spending much time at the beach. If he died, he wouldn't be spending much time anywhere.

When the sun began to set the guards collected him and marched him back to the operating theater he'd been in the day before. Oliver couldn't help but feel like a condemned man being taken to his place of execution. Part of him wanted to make a break for it and see how far he could get, but he knew from prior experience he wouldn't even make it to the first bend in the hallway before the cyborgs dropped him. Their weapons had a stun setting that he'd been on the wrong end of before. It didn't damage his body, but it left him immobile for the better part of half an hour. On top of that, it hurt like hell.

The guards pushed him into the room and shut the door behind him, leaving him alone. Oliver glanced over at the mirror where he knew the cyborgs would be observing him. "Screw you guys," he said.

There was no response. A moment later the door opened again and Maria stepped through. She was bound in exactly the same way she had been the day before, hands cuffed behind her back and arms chained to her sides. Three cyborgs in armor accompanied her, two holding her arms to guide her and the third carrying a scalpel at his side.

Two of the cyborgs propelled Maria forward, directly at

Oliver, who quickly found himself backed against a wall. The vampire looked at him curiously. "What *are* you?"

Oliver swallowed hard. "How do you mean?"

"Your blood…I've never felt like that before."

"Well, thanks, I guess."

A speaker on the wall crackled with static and a voice said, "Begin the experiment."

"What time is it?" Maria asked.

"Um…" Oliver said. "I don't know."

"Is it after sunset?"

"Oh. Yeah, the sun was going down when they brought me in here, so it'd have set by now."

"Good." She leaned forward. "I'm going to need a distraction," she whispered, "so make this look good."

"Make what look…" Oliver began, but the vampire sank her fangs into his neck before he could finish the sentence. Pain shot through his body again. Unlike the regular needle jabs the cyborgs had put him through, Oliver doubted this was the kind of thing a person could ever get used to.

Maria took one good swallow and then pulled back. She sighed deeply and licked her lips. "I don't think I could live on that," she noted, "but it would be nice to have once in a while. Like a really good Cognac."

Oliver blinked twice and shook his head to clear it. The vampire had taken much less blood this time; he didn't feel nearly as dizzy as before. Still, it wasn't an experience he'd choose to repeat.

Maria nodded at the cyborg with the scalpel. "Now," she said. "Like I told you."

The cyborg stepped forward and drew the blade across her neck in a quick, clean motion. Blood welled up in a line on her skin. She smiled at Oliver. "Come give me a kiss."

The cyborg who had been holding the scalpel put it away and seized Oliver, forcing his head forward until his lips were touching Maria's wound. He felt her blood seeping between his lips and into his mouth. It was room temperature rather than warm, but sweet and spicy with none of the metallic taste he might have expected. He couldn't help but take a swallow. "Now remember," she cooed, "give me that distraction."

Oliver's stomach did a flip-flop and he suddenly felt sharp pains in his abdomen, as if he'd swallowed a handful of razor blades. He pulled back from the vampire, who watched him with interest. The three cyborgs did the same. Oliver took a deep breath; he felt his body heating up with fever and sweat began to form on his forehead. It was similar to the way he felt when his body was rejecting the cyborg nanobots, but far more intense. His body was no more receptive to vampire blood than it had been to those tiny machines.

Oliver leaned forward, retching once, and then vomited the blood and the contents of his stomach onto the operating theater's clean tile floor. Tendrils of smoke rose from the blood, and then the blood itself caught fire as if someone had dropped a match onto a pool of red gasoline.

Maria watched the small blaze for a brief moment. "Good distraction," she said. Then she jerked her arms outward and the handcuffs and chains binding her arms snapped as if they'd been made out of silly string. She turned in one quick motion and seized the nearest cyborg's head, yanking it sharply to the side until his neck snapped. Before Oliver even registered what had happened she drove her fist through the next cyborg's chest plate, rooting around for a moment before tearing his heart out through his ribcage. She held the heart up so the third cyborg could see it, then reached out and twisted his head around so far it was facing in the opposite direction. Oliver heard a loud snap, and then Maria pulled the head right off of the cyborg's body.

The cyborg bodies had hit the ground before Oliver fully realized what was going on. "What are you doing?"

"I'm Luke Skywalker. I'm here to rescue you," Maria said. Then she turned and hurled the severed cyborg head through the mirror that led to the observation room. The glass shattered like it had been hit with a mallet, revealing half a dozen cyborgs standing there.

"We seem to have underestimated the vampire's strength," SCI-3422XB noted. Maria was through the broken mirror half a second later. The next few seconds looked to Oliver like what might happen if six cyborgs got caught in some kind of industrial blender. Maria came back through the mirror once she'd finished with them, absently tossing a severed cyborg arm aside.

"We should probably get going," she said.

Oliver stared at her. "You're *Luke Skywalker*?"

The vampire shrugged. "Your friends told me to say that so you'd trust me. It's quicker than explaining all of this to you. Now let's go." She took an assault rifle off one of the cyborg corpses. "Do you have any idea how to use this?"

Oliver took the gun and examined it. The cyborgs had brought their own weaponry when they'd invaded Earth, but the basic principles looked the same. "It fires energy bolts," he said. He raised the gun and looked down the barrel. "As long as it's just pulling the trigger, sure. But where exactly are we going to go? They control the entire west coast, unless you're thinking of the San Diego Resistance?"

"We only have to get as far as Filbert Street."

"What's on Filbert Street?"

The vampire stopped to pick a bit of skin out of her teeth, examining it for a moment before dropping it to the floor. "Look, I'm not going to pretend I understand any of this, but your people have a way to fix everything. I didn't remember any of the last year, I mean the *real* last year, until they found me."

"The *real*...hang on. Who sent you? Who are these people?"

Maria looked into his eyes. "You really don't remember any of this, do you? Artemis? That twisted bitch Sally Rain?" Oliver shook his head. "Not even that talking cat you hang around with?"

"No, I...*talking cat*?"

"Forget it. Let's go." Maria turned and started for the door. Oliver hesitated for a moment, then followed her. He had very little else in the way of options, he thought. Even if he was captured, he'd only find himself back in the same situation he'd been in an hour ago. Unless the cyborgs just decided to kill him, which was probably inevitable, anyway.

Maria eschewed bringing an assault rifle of her own, but

moved so quickly in the face of danger that her hands were probably more effective than any weapon she could have brought, anyway. Two cyborg sentries met a quick end in the first hallway they entered almost before Oliver had even noticed they were there, and much less before he'd have had time to think about raising his weapon and firing at them. A moment later he found himself watching as Maria flattened the skull of another cyborg up against a wall. "I'm surprised you don't...you know."

Maria wiped cyborg blood off of her face. "What?"

"Eat them."

"Only when I absolutely have to." She made a face. "They taste *awful*. It's those little machines in their blood."

"I guess we're lucky they can't convert you."

"*You* certainly are."

Oliver followed the vampire down a series of corridors. The medical center was largely deserted, which Oliver took as a hopeful sign. He hadn't been outside the grounds since he'd been brought here, but could only hope the rest of the city would be similarly empty. SCI-3422XB had told him that most of the city's converted population was involved in the war effort, and that only an occupation force had remained behind. He had no idea how large that force might be, but if they were lucky maybe they could get as far as Filbert Street before anyone noticed them. "How do you plan to get out of here?"

"I thought we'd steal an ambulance," Maria said. She stopped at a set of double doors. "Through here."

Oliver wasn't entirely surprised to find the ambulance bay unoccupied. The cyborgs had no need to guard a fleet of vehicles they had no use for. Maria chose an ambulance near the exit. "Now how do these open?" she asked, examining the closed garage doors.

"Maybe with this," Oliver pressed a switch next to the orange doors, which began to retract into the ceiling. He only had a brief moment to feel pleased with himself, though, before an alarm began blaring through the building. The carnage Maria had left in her wake hadn't gone unnoticed.

"Damn it," the vampire said. "I needed two more minutes. We should probably leave now."

Oliver wasn't about to argue. He climbed into the passenger side of the ambulance as Maria took the wheel. "I don't see the keys," he noted.

Maria ripped a panel off from under the steering column and began fiddling with the wires there. "You know how to hotwire a car?" Oliver asked.

"I've been a vampire for almost two hundred years. I know lots of things," Maria said. The ambulance's engine sputtered once and then roared to life. "See?"

"I opened the garage," Oliver said just a bit defensively.

"I'm so proud of you." Maria examined the instrument panel. "Half a tank of gas. That's more than enough." She put the ambulance into gear and started forward.

Two armed cyborgs appeared at the garage door and raised their weapons. Maria gunned the ambulance and ran them over. Oliver winced at the thudding noises as the bodies passed underneath the vehicle's tires. "We may be in some trouble," Maria said. "I didn't think they'd find us that fast."

"How much trouble?"

They turned onto Divisadero Street and started north toward Filbert. "About that much," she said, nodding at something outside the windshield.

Oliver looked. The area they were passing through had been cleared of cars, but he suspected the cyborgs had done that to make it easier for their tanks to pass through the narrow streets. He was fairly certain of this because he saw two of the tanks now, springing into action ahead of them. One of them fired a shell at them but missed, exploding a nearby tree. "How far do we have to go?"

"Too far." Maria hit the gas pedal and the ambulance's tires screeched. Several cyborgs appeared behind the tanks, weapons trained on them.

"We're going *through* them?"

"Unless you have a better idea?"

The cyborgs opened fire with their energy weapons. One shot hit a front tire and the ambulance lurched to the left. Maria managed to recover and aimed for a spot between the tanks. Unfortunately for the cyborgs, this put them directly in her path. Two of them found themselves run down, while a third was knocked onto their hood as they sped past the tanks. He began crawling toward them, seeming to mean to come through the windshield to get at them. Maria slammed on the brakes and sent the cyborg hurtling forward, rolling down the street like a bowling ball. She hit the gas again but the ambulance was hit by energy weapons fire several more times. Oliver could see electricity arcing all around them and a smell like burning metal began to filter through his nostrils.

Filbert Street was only a few blocks up Divisadero. Maria managed to make the turn at the right intersection, but the ambulance chose that moment to die on them. She tried to restart the vehicle once before giving up. "Out!"

Outside the ambulance, Oliver took a look around. He could hear metal treads grinding on the pavement in the distance; the tanks were coming after them. He was fairly certain he heard a helicopter on its way, as well. "At least we're on Filbert Street," he said.

"Filbert is *long*," Maria said. "Your friends are monitoring their communications. With any luck they'll be on their way to pick us up."

Oliver still didn't know who his "friends" were supposed to be, but that was about the least pressing thing on his mind at the moment. Now he could hear the march of boots coming in their direction. Cyborgs never ran anywhere. They didn't need to. Like the zombies on television shows, they somehow seemed to know that their prey couldn't run away forever.

"Up Filbert," Maria said. "Let's move."

They began running up Filbert Street, Oliver wishing he had something on his feet besides hospital slippers. He was almost grateful they didn't have to worry about what they'd look like to anyone passing by. Two people who looked like escapees from a mental hospital would draw more than passing attention even on a normal day in San Francisco. But the reality of the situation was worse. The fact that one of them was clearly still human and the other could pass for one if the sun wasn't burning her to cinders would stand out like a sore thumb to any cyborg that spotted them. "How far are we going?" Oliver panted.

"Russian Hill," Maria said. Oliver's heart sank. The Russian Hill neighborhood was on the other side of Van Ness, which itself was at least twelve blocks from their current position.

"We'll never make it that far."

"Hopefully we don't need to."

A spotlight beamed down on them from overhead. Oliver looked up and saw that the helicopter he'd heard before had found them. A moment later headlights swung around the corner at Baker Street behind them and two black SUVs headed in their direction. The sound of marching boots was louder now, and seemed to be coming from either side.

Maria stopped. "This would be a really good time for your friends to show up," she noted.

Oliver would have had to agree, even without knowing who those friends were. This would be a good time for *anything* to happen that didn't involve being captured or killed. Cyborgs never got angry, so they wouldn't just execute him out of spite, but they might well calculate he simply wasn't worth the trouble of keeping alive anymore.

The SUVs stopped a dozen feet away and the cyborgs inside piled out, weapons pointing at Oliver and Maria. "Do not attempt to resist," one said. "Resistance is…"

"Futile?" Oliver asked.

The cyborg considered that. "I was going to say *useless*, but you seem to have grasped the general idea."

"Start running," Maria said. "I'll deal with them and catch up with you."

Oliver looked up Filbert Street. He couldn't imagine he'd ever make it to Russian Hill before the cyborgs cut him off. But now he saw something coming *down* Filbert toward them.

It was difficult to see at first, but there was definitely…

"What the *hell*?" Oliver asked.

Maria followed his gaze up the street. "Oh," she said. "There's that good timing I was hoping for."

Oliver was having trouble believing he wasn't actually having some kind of very strange nightmare. Running directly toward him was what at first glance appeared to be Chewbacca. The creature was tall, covered with brown hair, and roaring at the top of its lungs. But its head wasn't that of a friendly Wookiee. It appeared to have the head of a fierce-looking wolf.

"That's it," Oliver said. "I'm done. I'm just done."

"What do you mean?" Maria asked.

"That's the goddamn Wolfman."

"No," Maria said. "The Wolfman isn't real. But it *is* a werewolf."

The werewolf roared, giving Oliver a chance to take in two rows of razor-sharp teeth. Three cyborgs coming up the street to intercept them opened fire on it, but the werewolf shrugged off the energy bolts, merely howling in pain rather than dropping to the ground in paralyzed agony as Oliver would have done. All of Oliver's instincts told him to run away as the werewolf ran directly toward him, but his legs stayed firmly rooted in the ground. Was there any chance he was really locked away in an asylum somewhere, and that all of this was a crazy man's fantasy?

The werewolf reached Oliver and scooped him up in a fireman's carry. "Hey!" Oliver shouted. He beat at the werewolf's back with his hands. "Put me down!"

Oliver could see more cyborgs approaching; there had to be twenty or more on foot now and the tanks weren't far away. "Take him," he heard Maria say. "I'll keep them busy for as long as I can." The werewolf whined at her. "It's okay," she said. "Just *fix* this, Tyler. Save the world."

The werewolf turned back the way he'd come and began running up Filbert with Oliver over his shoulder, loping his way along with long strides that Oliver could never have matched. The SUVs could have caught them easily enough, but from his position Oliver could see Maria charging them, screaming like a banshee. She went to work on the cyborgs with her hands and was quickly lost in a sea of bodies and flying body parts.

The werewolf kept running. Above them, the helicopter's searchlight caught them as they crossed Buchanan Street. Oliver would have had to admit the werewolf was making good time to Russian Hill. Had it also *run* all the way to meet them? It must have. Not getting tired had its advantages.

A cyborg squad attempted to intercept them at Van Ness, but the werewolf used its free arm to bat two of them away. Another managed to catch him square in the chest with an energy bolt and the werewolf roared, staggering for just a moment, then recovered and continued running. Oliver's body had gone numb from what little of the weapon's energy he'd been unfortunate enough to absorb in the blast. Things were going to take a bad turn for him once the cyborgs stopped trying to capture them and set their weapons to kill rather than stun.

Filbert Street turned into a long hill after crossing Van Ness. It was far from the steepest incline in the city, but Oliver knew walking the rest of the way to Russian Hill would have worn him out in short order. In his defense he'd have pointed out that he hadn't had any real exercise in months, ever since the cyborgs had taken him prisoner. In all honesty, though, he'd have had a rough time with it even before that. The werewolf barely seemed to notice the incline, though. It didn't even appear to be breathing hard as they crossed Larkin Street. It occurred to Oliver that riding by werewolf, as bizarre as it was, was probably still faster than taking a taxi would have been in San Francisco in the days before the cyborgs had come.

A second airborne searchlight joined the first. Oliver doubted it would be long before the cyborgs had them surrounded again, and it was unlikely they'd ask him to surrender before opening fire this time. He was about to tell the werewolf they might try hiding instead of running when it stopped suddenly and stepped into an empty lot. Somewhere in the back of his mind, Oliver wondered why there was an empty lot on Filbert Street. For as long as he'd lived in the city, Oliver couldn't remember a lot east of Van Ness staying vacant for long. There was simply too little real estate, and this was a prime area. He might have spent more time trying to puzzle that out, but he was keenly aware that the werewolf was no longer running. "Are we giving up?" he asked. He wasn't sure how he was going to explain this werewolf business to the cyborgs, provided they didn't just shoot him first.

The werewolf advanced a few steps into the lot, then reached out one paw as if it were opening a door. Oddly enough, Oliver could actually hear a door opening. Then the werewolf stepped forward, and what had been an empty lot shimmered and became the interior of a house. The werewolf turned and shut the door behind them.

Oliver attempted not to collapse in shock as the werewolf put him down. There had been no house on this lot. He'd seen it standing vacant when he'd been outside. But now here he was inside one. It wasn't a great deal to look at; he was in a sparsely decorated living room. Edwardian chairs sat around a wooden table that had several old-looking books on top of it. A teapot sat on a silver tray nearby, with several delicate cups at the ready. A staircase along one wall led up to another level. As Oliver looked around he didn't see any family photos or other decorations that made the place look as if somebody lived here. It looked like a model home more than anything else.

"What the hell *is* this?" Oliver asked.

A blonde girl of about ten years old emerged from the kitchen carrying a muffin on a small square plate. She wore jeans and a t-shirt with a *Pokémon* character on the front. She looked Oliver up and down, then glanced at the werewolf. "I cannot help but notice that Maria is not with you."

The werewolf whined and shook its head. Oliver didn't know how sad a werewolf was capable of looking, but this one certainly seemed unhappy.

The girl sighed. "A pity. We could have used the help. Do not mourn her, Mr. Jacobsen. If we succeed in our mission, she will be restored to life as if this never happened." She frowned. "Well, not *life*, precisely. She is a vampire, after all." The werewolf whined again and looked at the waiting teapot meaningfully. "You will not handle my china until you have resumed your human form," the girl said.

"Excuse me?" Oliver asked. "What is this? Who are you?"

The little girl nodded at him. "Mr. Jones. It is agreeable to see you again after all this time."

"All this time?" Oliver took a step forward but his legs suddenly felt weak and he nearly tripped. "We've never met," he said, bracing his hands on his knees for support.

"Of that you are mistaken," the girl said, "but you are forgiven for being unable to remember. You will probably want to sit down for what is about to happen." The werewolf took Oliver by the arm and led him to one of the chairs. Oliver sat down hard, his head beginning to spin.

"What's happening?" Oliver asked. "What did you do?"

"Nothing at all, Mr. Jones," the girl replied. "It is rather this house that is affecting you. It exists in its own timeline, you see, and is now restoring you to yours. The correct timeline, that is. I fear the process can be somewhat unpleasant, though."

For a moment Oliver thought he saw the walls of the house starting to melt, and then his vision snapped back into focus. One moment he was sitting in the chair and the next the chair was gone, but he was still sitting as if it hadn't moved at all. And then the chair was back. For a brief moment he caught sight of another woman, a redhead with a stern expression, who marched down the stairs and then out the front door, slamming it behind her. A moment later he saw another little girl who could have been the first one's twin, but this one was wearing a Girl Scout uniform, and then she vanished as well.

He heard a rustling and looked at the stairs. A small cat ran down the steps and made a beeline for him, leaping onto his lap and purring with wild enthusiasm. Oliver couldn't remember anyone ever being so happy to see him before. "Hi there," he said, scratching the cat behind the ears.

"Hey, boss," the cat said. "I sure missed you."

Oliver stared at the cat in disbelief. "Aw, hell," he said. Werewolves and vampires were hard enough to deal with. A talking cat was where he drew the line.

Then his vision filled with stars. The last thing he remembered before passing out was seeing the werewolf reaching for the teapot, only to have the little girl slap its paw away.

Chapter 14

Oliver had, to the best of his recollection, had only one dream in his life. It had been while he'd been on the run from the Kalatari, when his entire life had been undergoing a radical change. He'd assumed that his brain had needed to dream in order to cope with what was going on back then.

He was aware that people often said that everyone had dreams all the time and just forgot them, but prior to that one time he didn't have a single memory of dreaming at any other point in his life. He'd asked a doctor about it once during a routine physical, wondering if maybe something could be wrong with him. His doctor had told him not to worry about it. At the time, Oliver had doubted the doctor actually believed him.

Now he was dreaming again. That much he was certain of. He dreamed that he'd been in his office at the hedge fund six months ago when a man claiming to be an investigator with the SEC had visited, asking to interview him about some government matter. That man had turned out to be an assassin hired by the Kalatari to kill him. His life had been saved by Tyler Jacobsen, who had arrived with only seconds to spare. Tyler was a tall man with a fondness for Hawaiian shirts, who just happened to be a werewolf. He'd met and been punched by Sally Rain, a fiery redhead who was as deadly with her two pistols as anyone Oliver had ever seen. They both worked for Artemis, who physically appeared to be a ten-year-old girl. She'd been wearing a Girl Scout uniform the first time Oliver had met her. Artemis was not ten years old, however. Nobody on the team knew how old she truly was, but Oliver was willing to guess it was somewhere in the thousands of years.

When the episode with the Kalatari was over, Artemis had offered him a job, and he'd taken it. He'd simply seen too many things to go back to his old, boring life. He'd known then that he'd never be the same.

And then there was Jeffrey, his cat. Jeffrey had been a stray that Oliver had taken to feeding. Through means he didn't understand, Oliver had given him the power to speak. Jeffrey could be a bit of a pain, but Oliver loved him. He wasn't just a pet anymore; he was a friend.

In his dream his friends had been searching for him, knowing that he was a prisoner of the cyborgs. Artemis had promised to find him, and Artemis was the kind of person who took promises very seriously. She would have given up at nothing to keep her word.

Oliver opened his eyes. He was still in the living room of the house the werewolf had carried him to, but now he recognized his surroundings. This was the house in Russian Hill where time stood still. It couldn't even be seen from the outside if you didn't know how to look for it. The only explanation Oliver had been given was that the house existed at a fixed point in time. It would always be here, unchanged, regardless of whatever was happening outside it.

Tyler sat in another chair, no longer in wolf form. He'd changed into one of his myriad Hawaiian shirts. Oliver had wondered in the past how many of those shirts Tyler owned. Every time he "wolfed out" whatever clothes he was wearing at the time were torn apart. He suspected Tyler shopped in bulk.

Tyler perked up when he saw Oliver awake. "How are you feeling, buddy?"

Oliver had a splitting headache. "Like I got blackout drunk last night."

"Yeah. I get that." He took a sip from one of Artemis's teacups. "It wasn't pleasant for me, either, but you had it worse. You had longer to catch up on."

"Catch up?"

"To the right time."

Oliver shook his head. He'd been offered LSD once in college and turned it down. If the effects had been anything like this, he was glad he had.

Artemis entered the room carrying a tray with a bowl of steaming hot soup on top. Jeffrey followed her closely, watching the tray with barely-disguised intent. She put the tray down on the table next to Oliver while Jeffrey hopped up onto his lap. "You should eat, Mr. Jones."

"I'm not really hungry. I think I might be sick, actually."

"I can imagine you don't feel like eating, but you need your energy."

"I'll help you eat it," Jeffrey said. "It has chicken and shrimp."

Artemis took a third chair and studied Oliver's face. "Tell me. What do you remember?"

That was a question Oliver had been struggling with for the past few moments. "I remember another life."

Artemis nodded. "Let me be more specific. What is the very *last* thing you remember?"

"We were in the office. I had a hangover. There was a...*timequake*, you said. That's what you called it."

"Very good. And what happened then?"

Oliver looked around. "I woke up here. In this chair. But...I have *other* memories. There was a cyborg invasion. They took me prisoner and ran tests on me. Maria showed up and broke me out." He looked at Artemis. "Did I just *imagine* all of that?"

"No, not at all. That happened."

"But I also remember it *not* happening. I met you six months ago. There were no cyborgs. Not until that one in the parking garage who wanted to kill Sally." He looked around. "Where the hell *is* Sally?"

Tyler grimaced. "If she is still alive, she's back on her world," Artemis said. "While her deception of you was, in some respects, quite clever, her plan on the whole was remarkably stupid."

"Her plan?"

"She tried to change the past," Tyler said.

"Changing the past is bad news!" Jeffrey intoned dramatically. "It is the one thing you must *never* do!" Oliver stared at the cat in surprise. "I've been cooped up in here for weeks," Jeffrey said. "I learned all about this stuff."

"Weeks?" Oliver asked.

"It is a bit of a long story, Mr. Jones," Artemis said. "In some respects, I am a bit like this house. Time does not affect me in that same way it affects other things. However, I do know when time is *wrong*. I recognized the timeline fracture when the cyborgs crossed over and I activated our contingency plan, which was for all team members to come to this house in order that they would be restored to their correct timelines."

"Okay…"

"Being a fixed point in time, the house is unconcerned with what goes on outside. It only cares about its own timeline, which happens to be the same as ours. When you came inside, your memories of the correct timeline were restored, even though that timeline does not currently exist."

"Are you saying the house is *conscious*?" Oliver asked.

"Not in any sense you would understand consciousness," Artemis said.

"Are you confused yet?" Tyler asked.

"Yes," Oliver said.

"Try to keep up, boss," Jeffrey said.

"You're the expert now?" Oliver asked the cat.

"Compared to you I'm the Doctor."

Oliver was beginning to rethink Jeffrey's television

privileges. Letting an intelligent cat watch *Doctor Who* might not be the best idea. He might start getting dangerous ideas. He looked back at Artemis. "So what's going on outside? Are the cyborgs gone?"

"No. At this very moment they are attempting to locate you and Mr. Jacobsen. They should lack the capacity to discern the existence of this house, however."

"But what if they do...*discern* the existence of this house?"

Artemis shrugged. "I truly do not know. In the house's timeline they never existed on this planet, so they might simply cease to exist if they cross into it. Or the entire universe might explode. I am fairly certain it would be one or the other."

"Oh," Oliver said. "Of course." He looked around. "Where's Seven?"

"Dead," Tyler said. "They got him when Santa Fe fell. The rest of us barely made it out of there."

"But I thought you came straight here..."

"We were not *in* San Francisco at the time of the invasion," Artemis said. "Getting here took a great deal of time and work, and was not without significant losses."

"Oh. I'm sorry." Seven hadn't been the cuddliest person Oliver had ever met, but he'd liked the man. The others had worked with him for far longer, of course.

"It is no matter," Artemis said. "He will be restored when we correct the timeline. Everything will go back to the way it was."

"And the others come back, too," Tyler said. "Maria. God, we really could have used her."

"So you brought her here?" Oliver asked. "She knew who I was, so obviously you did. How did you recruit her?"

"She was on a one woman, or I guess one *vampire* mission to destroy the cyborgs after they killed John Blackwell and the others," Tyler said.

"They got the vampires," Oliver said quietly.

"Oh, yeah. They went down fighting, though. Blackwell's group took an entire battalion of cyborgs with them but in the end they were just too outnumbered. Maria got away and was still out there ripping heads off every night. We brought her here and she got her memories of the world where Blackwell didn't die. She said she'd do anything for us if it meant fixing the timeline and getting her master back."

"And I was there, too," Jeffrey said.

"You were with the vampires?" Oliver asked, surprised.

"No," Jeffrey said. "I was a few blocks away hunting for mice. Those damn robot people never throw anything away, so leftover food got pretty scarce. That dog," he nodded at Tyler, "scooped me up and brought me in here. I don't mind telling you I was pretty freaked out when I found out there were human dogs."

"He scratched the shit out of me," Tyler said.

"But then once I got inside here, I got my memories back and I could talk and think again. It was pretty great."

Oliver scratched the cat behind the ears. "Good job," he said. Jeffrey purred.

"Good job?" Tyler asked. "I'm the one who found him. And he never apologized for scratching me."

"Did someone say something?" Jeffrey asked. "I can't hear it when dogs talk."

"So what was Sally's plan?" Oliver asked Artemis. "I know she felt pretty bad about what she did to the cyborgs after the war. So…she went back in time and *didn't* kill them?"

"That would have been problematic enough," Artemis said. "It appears that she took the time machine back to a point before the mirror here had been destroyed, so that she was able to return home. But from Seven's analysis of the cyborgs we managed to capture before his death, we know that not only were the cyborgs not destroyed by the nanobot virus, but that the cure was never deployed, either. This leads me to believe Sally removed her sister from the research facility where she had been working on it."

"The facility where she died," Oliver said.

"Yeah," Tyler said. "With no cure, the cyborgs won. They probably took over the whole planet."

"And found the mirror there?" Oliver asked.

"We believe the mirror on their world was destroyed," Artemis said. "At some point before the invasion here we found we could no longer use ours to travel and assumed they'd lost the war. Besides, if the cyborgs had used it to get here, they would have been contained in Vault 3. However, if they analyzed the remains of their world's mirror, they may have incorporated some aspects of it into their developing teleportation technology."

"Which explains why they can move world-to-world but not place-to-place," Jeffrey said. "See? I really have been paying attention."

Oliver nodded. "It makes sense. Well, as much sense as any of this makes. They got close to us, like the cyborg that attacked Sally in the garage."

"*Indeed*," Jeffrey said. Oliver blinked at him in surprise. "That was my Artemis impression," the cat whispered loudly.

"If you're done?" Artemis asked.

"He's done," Oliver said. "So how do we fix any of this?"

"There is only one possibility," Artemis said, "as much as I detest it. We must stop Sally from changing the past. Once the timeline is set right in her world, ours will revert to normal."

"And how we do that?"

"It's kinda complicated," Tyler said.

Oliver resisted the urge to laugh. "More complicated than any of this?"

Artemis nodded. "We must go back in time, Mr. Jones. If we are to save our world, it is the only option open to us."

"We have to get back to Vault 3," Tyler said.

"You guys are screwed," Jeffrey said.

Chapter 15

Oliver had an idea where this conversation was going. "You want to go get the time machine," he said. "We're going after Sally?" Artemis nodded. "Why do you even think it's still there?"

"The time machine itself does not move," Artemis said. "It has no form of propulsion. It will be exactly where Sally left it."

"Then it's still in Santa Clara. Okay. You do realize that's an hour away from here by freeway? And that's on a good day."

"I do recall the location of the vault, Mr. Jones."

"It's impossible," Oliver said. "We barely made it here from Geary Street, and that's only about 30 blocks or so. How are we going to get to Santa Clara? How did you even get here from...wherever you were."

"We had help," Tyler said. "The San Diego Resistance fighters are some serious badasses."

"So they're around here somewhere waiting for us?"

"No," Artemis said. "While I was able to convince Commander James to smuggle us into the city, it was with the caveat that it was a one-way trip."

"Then how?" Oliver asked.

"Perhaps I will perform one of my many miracles, Mr. Jones."

"I don't think sleight of hand is going to help us this time."

"We have a plan," Tyler said. "Check this out." He left his chair and went upstairs. When it was obvious he wasn't going to return immediately, Oliver took the time to eat some of the soup Artemis had brought for him. Jeffrey stared at the bowl longingly until Oliver bit a piece of shrimp in half and offered him some. Jeffrey downed it with much gusto.

"This really is good," Oliver said to Artemis.

"Inform Mr. Jacobsen of your approval," she said. "It is another of his family recipes. There are also muffins in the kitchen for you to enjoy." Oliver nodded. He'd get to those in a minute. Tyler also happened to be an excellent baker.

After about ten minutes Tyler came back down the stairs, now dressed in a black bodysuit covered with cyborg armor plating. He turned around once so Oliver could get a good look. The suit was remarkably convincing, although Tyler lacked the glowing blue eye all cyborgs had. Oliver pointed that out and Tyler shrugged. "It's not perfect, but from a distance it'll fool them. I've made a couple trips out wearing it without anyone looking twice."

"You see?" Artemis asked. "Dressed in this manner, you should have no problems finding a vehicle. With it, we will make the trip to the vault."

Oliver thought it over. "I haven't seen any cyborgs your size," he said to Artemis.

"There are none," she said. "They do not convert children, as they find the physical growth that is typical in younger humans incompatible with the process. Rather, children are held in guarded facilities until they are fully grown. Once they determine that physical maturation is complete, the conversion process is initiated."

Oliver had trouble believing what he was hearing. "Are you saying they have kids in *concentration camps*?"

"I might have not chosen that terminology, but you are not incorrect." She sipped her tea. "You are thinking of liberating them, of course. Tyler felt the same way. Put that thought from your mind. We have no more use for children than the cyborgs do."

Oliver's mouth dropped open. "Did you really just say that?" he asked. "That's...that's *inhuman*."

Artemis stared at him. "And what exactly do you think I am, Mr. Jones?"

"I don't know. You won't tell me."

"Not today. Perhaps I will tomorrow. One never knows. Calm yourself, Mr. Jones. Understand that when we fix the timeline, those *camps* will never have existed."

"I didn't like it either, Oliver, but it makes sense," Tyler said. "The only way to save everyone is by keeping this whole thing from happening in the first place."

Oliver went to the front window and looked outside. Two

cyborgs stood in the street less than a dozen feet away, staring directly at him. Oliver jerked, but the cyborgs had no reaction to his presence. After a moment they turned away and began marching down Filbert Street in the direction Oliver had come from.

"They really can't see us in here," Oliver said.

"Nope," Jeffrey said, coming up behind him. "Sometimes I get up there and put my butt on the glass. 'Look at my butt, you jerks!' I say." Oliver gave him a skeptical look. "What else am I going to do?" the cat asked. "I'm stuck in here all day. I get bored."

"If we may return to the subject, we will not need a suit for me," Artemis said. "You and Tyler will obtain and operate the vehicle. I can stay hidden inside until we reach Santa Clara. Once at the vault, it will be irrelevant whether they become aware of our presence. When we are below ground, I will destroy the access point, if need be. Even if any cyborgs should manage to make it inside, the security system there will be more than they can easily deal with. It is quite efficient."

"If you destroy the elevator we'll be trapped down there," Oliver said.

"If we fail in our mission, it will not matter much whether we are trapped or not."

Oliver found that difficult to argue with. "I suppose you have another one of those suits for me?"

"Upstairs," Tyler said. "Well, we'll have to put one together, I mean. We have a lot of parts lying around." He frowned. "You know, it seems like there should have been a more delicate way to say that."

"You have *parts*?" Oliver asked.

"Maria amused herself by hunting at night," Artemis said. "She did need to eat, after all, although she killed rather more of them than she required for sustenance, and the killings were quite...I suppose the word I am looking for is *dramatic.*"

"She was pretty pissed off," Tyler said. "She took John Blackwell's death really hard."

"I heard her crying sometimes," Jeffrey said. "She was sad a lot. I let her pet me, even though she was a dark fiend of the night."

Oliver reached down to scratch the cat. "That was very nice of you."

"I *know*. Her hands were *cold.*"

"In any case, Maria brought us a variety of pieces we will be able to use to provide you with a suitable disguise," Artemis said.

"You know how sometimes I bring you a dead mouse and you get all cranky?" Jeffrey asked. "Some people *like* when you bring them presents."

"It's not quite the same thing," Oliver said.

"I don't see how it's not," the cat noted. "You could wear the mouse as a little hat, if you wanted to. I don't judge."

"We have their weapons, too," Tyler said. "As long as we don't get too close to anyone, we'll be able to pass as a patrol."

Oliver sighed. "Okay. So when are we going to do this?"

"Tomorrow," Artemis said. "Things will have quieted down outside by then, once the cyborgs have directed their search for you and Mr. Jacobsen elsewhere. Tonight you should eat and get some rest. Things are about to become rather more complicated for us."

"That may be the understatement of the century," Oliver said.

"Not at all, Mr. Jones. I believe the understatement of the century was…" she trailed off. "Never mind. It hardly seems relevant right now. Finish your soup, Mr. Jones."

"Did she tell you I made muffins?" Tyler asked.

"Yeah. I think I'll go grab one…"

"Soup first, Mr. Jones," Artemis said sternly.

Oliver ate his soup.

Chapter 16

The next morning dawned foggy and cold. Oliver stood at the living room window as he sipped his morning tea. No cyborgs passed by outside, and he couldn't see anything overhead to indicate the area was still being searched. If the cyborgs were still looking for a werewolf carrying a man in a hospital gown, they were doing it somewhere else. It increased their odds of success, Oliver thought, if only by a little bit. At this point, though, he was willing to take what he could get.

When breakfast was finished Oliver and Tyler dressed up as cyborgs. Tyler had his own suit ready, and Oliver had a wide assortment of pieces to choose from; the room Maria had been sleeping in looked like an abattoir. Jeffrey watched them closely. "You guys look ridiculous," he said.

"The real question is do we look like cyborgs?" Oliver asked. He turned around once as if he were modeling new clothes. "What do you think?"

"I'd run away if I saw you coming," the cat said.

"That's good, I suppose."

"It would be because I'd be afraid if I didn't, I'd die laughing."

Oliver sighed. "They don't convert animals, do they?" Tyler asked.

"Not yet. I hope we're not next. I wouldn't like being a cyborg cat very much."

"You never know," Oliver said. "You didn't like being a *talking* cat at first, but you got used to it. You could get a little suit of armor. You might like it."

"You're mean," Jeffrey said. "If your bed was here, I'd pee on it."

Artemis was waiting for them downstairs when they were finished, another one of Tyler's muffins in her hand. She looked them up and down. "You look acceptable," she said. "I remember chastising Maria for bringing her work home with her, but in hindsight, I am glad she did. The assortment of pieces she collected saves us the trouble of going out to find new ones."

"That's one way of looking at it," Oliver said.

"With their weapons, which Maria also favored us with, you should be able to pass as a patrol unit to any casual observers. I would prefer it if we could do something about your eyes, but it cannot be helped. Avoid any close contact with others and you should have no trouble. Remember to walk, and remain emotionless. I don't want you two cracking each other up while you're marching down the street."

"Yes, mom," Tyler said. Artemis stared at him until he looked away. "Sorry."

Oliver glanced at the door. "How is it we won't forget about all of this the minute we're out there? I'm not going to go back to thinking a vampire just busted me out of the hospital?"

"Given a lengthy enough exposure, you might. Mr. Jacobsen did not remember ever meeting you until he came inside the house for the first time. However, his excursions outside afterward had no effect on his restored memories. Nor did those of Maria. It appears that once you have been placed back in your original timeline, it is difficult to pull you out of it. I would avoid taking any vacations, though. Get a vehicle and return here at once."

"Where should we look?" asked Oliver.

"The cyborgs use modified SUVs and Humvees pretty exclusively," Tyler said. "It shouldn't be that hard to find one if we just march around for a while."

"Pier 27," said Jeffrey. Everyone turned to stare at him. "What?" the cat asked. "I was outside, too. There's a bunch of stuff parked down there."

"How do you even know where Pier 27 is?" Oliver asked.

"You think I can't read signs? This coming from the guy who made me talk?"

"Fine." Oliver tried to imagine a map of San Francisco in his head. It had been a while since he'd driven anywhere without a GPS unit in his car. "That's right off of Lombard. We should be able to walk straight there."

"You sure you don't want me to just transform and run down there?" Tyler asked Artemis. "It would take me five minutes."

"If this house had a garage in which to hide it, perhaps," Artemis replied. "However, as it does not, I believe that if the cyborgs saw a werewolf steal one of their vehicles, they would likely give chase. And once it was parked outside, they would almost certainly take it back and resume searching this area."

"That does make sense," Tyler admitted.

"Good luck, both of you," Artemis said. "We will be waiting."

Oliver and Tyler stepped outside, assault rifles carried low as was normal for the cyborgs, and Oliver was shocked to see that time appeared to have stopped. Nothing outside moved and there was no sound, no wind, and nothing to indicate that he wasn't looking at a painting. "That's right," he said to Tyler. "I forgot about this. It takes a minute for the world to catch up to us. Or us to catch up to it." Oliver didn't know exactly which thing was true, but he'd had the same experience the first time he'd set foot outside this house six months ago. Everything would seem still at first, and then slowly begin moving again. The last time he'd done this he'd seen pedestrians frozen in mid-step, and he'd plucked a motionless leaf out of the sky as if he'd been pulling it out of tar.

"We've got a few minutes like this," Tyler said. "I made it halfway to Geary before things started moving again yesterday. Let's take advantage of it." They made a left turn and began walking up the hill.

They'd reached Grant Avenue and made the turn toward Lombard, passing one set of motionless cyborgs, before time slowly started catching up with them. In the distance Oliver could see more cyborgs slowly beginning to walk again, and a Humvee crossed the street ahead of them, seeming to speed up as it did so. By the time they reached Lombard things were back to normal. They turned right and began walking toward the water.

Oliver scanned the sky above them for any sign of helicopters, or anything else that might spot them. "Try not to look too interested in anything," Tyler said. "Remember, they just march when they're out on the streets."

"How am I supposed to keep an eye out, then?" Oliver asked.

"I don't know. Just look casual."

Oliver wasn't sure what a casual cyborg was supposed to look like, but he did his best not to look at any one thing for very long. As they marched another pair of cyborgs approached their position on the other side of the street.

"Are we supposed to wave at them or anything?" Oliver asked.

"I don't know," Tyler whispered back. "I never really spent a lot of time watching them. I was always kind of busy."

"Doing what?"

"Running away. Or killing them."

"Let's just ignore them."

They looked straight ahead as the other cyborgs passed by. The other two never gave them a second look. "Good," Tyler said. "Let's hope things stay that way."

"As long as nobody notices our eyes, we should be fine."

They walked until Lombard Street abruptly came to an end at the turnoff for Coit Tower. "Oh," Oliver said. "I guess it *doesn't* go all the way to the water." They could see down to the bay from their location at the top of the hill, but there was no easy way to get there. If they hadn't been trying to pass for cyborgs Oliver might have been willing to risk trying to pick their way down the hill, but that would look very odd to anyone who spotted them.

"Goddamn San Francisco," Tyler said. "Nothing about it makes any sense. Do you want to try Chestnut Street? That might go through."

"No, I think that one must end near those buildings," Oliver pointed into the distance. "We'll have to go up to Bay."

"I swear to god, I tried to get Artemis to move our office to Honolulu. 'Lots of crazy stuff happens there,' I said. 'Just look what happened to me!' But no…"

"Hawaii doesn't sound bad right now. Do you think the cyborgs made it that far?"

"They haven't yet. After the airports got shut down the military started shooting down anything that got close. Commander James said they've been trying ships but nothing's made it through the blockade."

They turned and began walking back down Lombard. "I can't believe we wasted that much time," Tyler said once they reached Bay Street. "Artemis is going to be pissed."

"As long as we get back with a car we'll be fine," Oliver said. "I'm surprised we haven't seen more cyborgs."

"Most of the ones in the city are working in the nutrient factories," Tyler said. "And a lot of them have gone to the battlefront. There's only a token force here, really."

"How many is that?"

"Maybe fifty thousand. But they're mostly on the other side of the city, near the ocean. There shouldn't be more than a few thousand around here."

"Nothing to worry about, then," Oliver grumbled. Then his eyes caught something strange and he stopped in his tracks. "What the hell is that?" he asked. Ahead of them, Oliver saw a patrol of four armed cyborgs crossing Kearney Street heading toward Fisherman's Wharf. That by itself didn't seem odd, but next to them he saw a girl in her late teens with long blonde hair skipping along beside them. She wore a green tank top with a golden ballerina skirt that reached to just below her knees. A pair of black ankle-high Doc Martens completed the outfit. While she clearly hadn't been converted, she showed no fear of the cyborgs whatsoever. "How do they not see her?"

Tyler followed his gaze up the street. "See who?"

Oliver pointed. "Her."

Tyler looked again. "I see cyborgs. That's all." He gave Oliver a worried look. "You okay, buddy?"

The girl skipped in a wide circle around the cyborgs, who ignored her entirely. Then she looked back at Oliver, gave him a cheerful wave, and disappeared with the cyborgs up Kearney Street.

"That was weird," Oliver said. "I swear I saw a girl with them."

"If there was a girl there, the cyborgs would have gotten her." Tyler frowned. "You may be having some kind of time thing."

"Time thing?"

Tyler shrugged. "I don't know. Maybe she was there at

some point in the past and that's what you're seeing. The past. Like a side effect from being in two different timelines."

"A *side effect*?"

"Give me a break. If you're worried about it, ask Artemis. But let's get moving. We're almost there."

There was significantly more cyborg activity down at the pier. As Jeffrey had said, plenty of vehicles were parked in the area, much of which had been razed and repaved with weapon turrets spaced along the waterfront at regular intervals. Oliver wasn't thrilled about the fact that it would remain impossible for them to go unseen, but as long as nobody got a close look they might still be okay. "Let's get a Humvee and get out of here."

The nearest one was parked half a block away, with one cyborg standing just outside the driver-side door. There were unguarded vehicles farther away, but that put them much closer to the rest of the cyborgs than Oliver cared to be. "Let's get that one," Tyler said.

"Do you think he's not going to notice when we steal his car?" Oliver asked.

"We'll improvise. Just act like a cyborg."

They marched up to the cyborg in as casual a manner as Oliver could imagine marching would look. The cyborg showed no interest in them as they approached. "What is your designation?" Oliver asked. He'd noticed the cyborgs always seemed fond of that question when they interacted.

"PT-8556BA. What is your designation?"

"SCI-3422XB," Oliver said. It was the only designation he knew off the top of his head. "We require this vehicle at the medical center. Please step aside."

The cyborg stepped aside without objection. Oliver could barely believe that had worked. "Carry on," he said, stepping toward the door.

"Hey, you used to work at that hamburger place in North Beach," Tyler said, suddenly perking up. "I knew I recognized you." Oliver winced. Cyborgs didn't get nostalgic about their old lives. A moment later Tyler winced, as well.

"That is irrelevant information," the cyborg said. "You appear to be malfunctioning." He took a closer look at Tyler. "No, it is not a malfunction. Your conversion process was unsuccessful. Allow me to assist you." He held up his arm and an injector unit slid out of a panel in his wrist guard.

Oliver stepped forward and shot the cyborg at point-blank range, then caught his body as he began to drop. Tyler helped him lay the cyborg down on the pavement. "Well, shit," Tyler said. "Do you think anyone saw that?"

"What has happened to PT-8556BA?" a voice asked from behind them. Oliver turned his head just enough to see a pair of cyborg boots.

"A malfunction," Oliver said. "We will take him in for maintenance."

"Yes, maintenance," Tyler agreed. "Maintenance is required for this unit."

"Clearly," the cyborg said. "Carry on."

Oliver continued pretending to inspect the fallen cyborg as the other one walked away. "Thank god they're idiots," Tyler said. "You'd think people being run by computers would catch on a little faster."

"They expect logic," Oliver said. "This is the least logical thing anyone has ever done. Let's stick him in the back and get out of here."

They lifted the cyborg by the arms and dragged him to the rear of the Humvee, then heaved him into the back. "It's a shame," Tyler said. "I loved those hamburgers."

"When we fix the timeline we'll go there and give him the biggest tip he's ever seen," Oliver said. "Let's get out of here."

The Humvee's keys were in the ignition. Oliver assumed that cyborgs didn't worry much about their vehicles being stolen. He switched it on. "Back the way we came? We're not going to run into any streets that don't go all the way there?"

"I think we could try Chestnut," Tyler said. "Oh, forget it. Better safe than we get stuck doing U-turns. Go up to Bay. It's farther but we won't get lost."

They managed to reach the house on Filbert Street without any complications. Artemis was waiting for them inside. "You took significantly longer than I expected," she noted, sipping a cup of tea.

"We got turned around," Oliver said.

"And we had to shoot a cyborg," Tyler added.

"I see. You were lucky, then. Anything else?"

Oliver considered telling her about the girl in the ballerina skirt, but this didn't seem like the right time for it. Maybe Tyler had been right and it was just some "time thing." The girl he'd seen had been entirely at ease with the cyborgs, though, and she'd definitely seen *him*. "It was fine," Oliver said.

"Good. I have packed some food." She nodded at a wicker

picnic basket near the door.

"Where did you get a picnic basket?" Oliver asked.

"It has been here since the 1920's," Artemis said. "I do not know who brought it here originally."

"Other people know about this place?" Oliver asked.

"It would seem so." Artemis shrugged. "In any case, if they return, I am certain they will not miss it after all this time. If you think you will be needing anything else, you should collect it now."

"I think we're all set," Tyler said.

Artemis looked at him. "Are you certain, Mr. Jacobsen, that you might not prefer to bring your standard clothing along with you? You will look like a walking target when we cross over to Sally's world."

"Good point," Tyler nodded. "I'll get yours, too, Oliver." He disappeared upstairs.

Jeffrey rubbed against the girl's ankles. "What am I supposed to do? I don't want to be alone."

"I do not think we will require your services. However, I will not stop you from joining us." Artemis frowned. "I do not recommend it, however."

"Why not?" the cat demanded. "You think I'll just get in the way? I think you're forgetting who kicked Dracula's ass. It sure wasn't these two knuckleheads."

"I had no doubt of your bravery. However, if we succeed in our mission, everything will be put right, and reality here will adapt. If we fail, we will likely be dead, and you will either join us in that fate or be trapped in a world even more unpleasant than this one, as hard to believe as that may sound."

"Oh," Jeffrey said.

"You're staying," Oliver said.

"But..."

"No," Oliver interrupted. "I'm putting my foot down here. If we don't come back and the world stays like this, you can go outside and find your girlfriend and still have as normal a life as anyone could expect."

"She's not really my *girlfriend*," Jeffrey said. "We had one dinner and then we went and made fun of dogs down at the park."

"You're staying here."

"Fine," Jeffrey said. "How long should I wait for you?"

"From your perspective, the change will be nearly instantaneous," Artemis said. "You should feel several timequakes..."

"Which is like an earthquake, but with time," Oliver said.

Artemis glanced at him. "Yes, that is one way of putting it. After that, things outside will shift dramatically. If after a few minutes nothing has changed, it never will."

"That sounds awfully final," Jeffrey said.

"Time travel is not without consequences," Artemis said. "Which is why it is forbidden."

Tyler came downstairs with his and Oliver's clothes neatly folded in his arms. "I have a couple extra guns, too," he said. "I don't know how many shots these things can get off before they need to be recharged, and it's not like we have anything to recharge them with."

"It will not hurt to have extra," Artemis nodded. "I do not expect a great deal of combat once we reach the other world, however. Their mirror was in Federation City, which should be relatively safe."

"Federation City?" Oliver asked.

"It occupies much the same location as Washington D.C. does here," Artemis said. "As I said before, in many ways that world will be indistinguishable from our own. In others, it is quite different. The American Federation rather than the United States, for example. They never had a civil war. A surprising number of people speak Esperanto…"

"Really?" Tyler asked. "I never knew that."

"It hardly seemed relevant to what we were doing at the time." Artemis finished her tea. "We have delayed long enough. Let us depart. We have quite a journey ahead of us."

Chapter 17

Saying goodbye to Jeffrey proved to be more difficult than Oliver had expected. As they prepared to depart the cat acted as if Oliver's ankles were made of Velcro. "You'll be okay, won't you?" he asked.

"I hope so," Oliver said. "Don't worry. You'll know pretty quick if things worked out. Just wait for the timequakes. You'll probably blink and suddenly be back in our house, wondering what I'm going to make you for dinner."

"Will I remember any of this?" the cat asked. "If it works, I mean?"

Oliver didn't honestly have any idea, but as always, Artemis wasn't far away. "Yes," she said. "You will each have another set of memories, but they will feel more like a dream than reality. You will remember a world in which the cyborgs came here and all of these things happened, but you will live in the world where they did not." She frowned slightly. "That is difficult to explain, but you will grow accustomed to it."

"You've done this before?" Oliver asked.

"Something similar," the girl said.

"Please don't die," Jeffrey said.

Oliver knelt down to scratch the cat's head. "I'll try my best, okay?"

"You can pick me up if you want to."

Oliver's eyes widened slightly. Jeffrey rarely wanted to be picked up, and usually that was just so he could see something better. He figured he might as well make the most of the opportunity, scooping the cat up and holding him close. "You take care of yourself, okay? If nothing here changes, I mean. Have a good long life."

"It won't be as good if you aren't around to cook me shrimp. Promise you'll make me shrimp when you get back?"

Oliver sighed. "I promise." He briefly considered kissing the cat on the top of his head, but decided that would be taking things too far. Jeffrey would never let him hear the end of it.

Once outside, Artemis balked at the idea of riding next to the dead cyborg in the Humvee. "It appears that your trip was indeed complicated," she noted.

"We were going to dump him somewhere," Tyler said.

"Dump him now," Artemis said. "We'll be far from here before a patrol finds him."

The trip out of San Francisco was fairly simple. Oliver found Van Ness without getting turned around and headed south out of the city. They passed several cyborg patrols on foot and a number of other vehicles, but for all intents and purposes he and Tyler appeared to be two cyborgs off on some cyborg business. They didn't attract so much as a second look.

Oliver hesitated when they reached the on-ramp to the freeway. "Is there a speed limit now?"

Tyler shrugged. "I haven't been on the freeway in a while. Just drive as fast as everyone else." Oliver gestured outside. The freeway was currently devoid of other vehicles. "I don't know," Tyler said. "Drive casual."

"Drive casual," Oliver muttered. "Fine." He nosed the Humvee up to 60 miles per hour and resolved to keep it there until they saw another car he could match speeds with.

The Humvee's instrument panel had been modified to include a console with digital readouts that Oliver was sure indicated *something* to the cyborgs, but he honestly couldn't tell what. It didn't seem to matter as far as operating the vehicle itself went, though. Driving was the same as it had always been.

The morning fog had burned off and while Oliver could see one helicopter overhead, it didn't appear to be taking any interest in them. With no traffic to impede them, they'd be able to make it to Santa Clara within an hour, as long as nothing went wrong.

It took half an hour for things to go wrong. Oliver heard a clicking noise and then a voice came through a speaker built into the cyborg instrument panel. "This vehicle is out of its designated operations area," it said. "What is your designation?"

Oliver and Tyler shared a worried look. "PT-8556BA?" the voice asked. "Are you operating this vehicle?"

"He's not here right now," Tyler said.

"Why didn't you just say *yes?*" Oliver whispered.

"What if they know him or something?" Tyler whispered back.

"Who is this?" the voice asked. "What is your designation?"

Oliver thought it over. "SCI-3422XB. I required this vehicle for…a special assignment."

It was nearly a minute before the voice replied. "SCI-3422XB was rendered inoperative. What is your correct designation?"

"No, it's definitely me," Oliver said. "SCI-3422XB. I'm fine now."

"He got better," Tyler volunteered. Oliver glared at him.

"I suggest you drive faster, Mr. Jones," Artemis said from the back seat. "I believe we will have company soon."

"What is your designation?" the voice asked again.

"Is there a way to shut this stupid thing off?" Tyler asked, fiddling with the controls on the instrument panel.

"Cease vehicle operation immediately and wait for contact," the voice commanded.

"I'd say shoot it, but you might kill the car and we'd be stranded here," Oliver said. "It's not worth the risk." He pushed the vehicle up to 80.

The voice over the speaker commanded them to stop the Humvee twice more before apparently giving up. They made it another ten minutes and then Tyler spotted a helicopter heading in their direction. "That one's spotted us," he said.

Oliver looked up. The helicopter was taking a position overhead. "Do you think they'll try and shoot us?"

"Not from there," Tyler said. "They'll want to see what we are before they blow us up."

"Well, I guess that's comforting," Oliver said. He checked the rear view mirror. Another Humvee had appeared behind them. This one didn't seem concerned with speed limits; it was gaining on their position rapidly. Oliver pressed the accelerator down as far as it would go. There was no point in pretending they were just cyborgs out on some business anymore.

The exit they needed for Santa Clara was still two miles away when Oliver saw four more Humvees in front of them. They'd parked in a V formation that looked like it was intended to form a roadblock. At least eight cyborgs stood in front of the vehicles, weapons trained on them. Oliver pulled the Humvee onto the shoulder and barreled past, just managing to squeeze through the gap between one of the other Humvee's bumpers and the crash barrier. Their Humvee was hit twice by weapons fire and Oliver felt his hands tingling as the energy dissipated around them. The vehicle's interior lights flickered and for a moment Oliver thought it might die on them, but the engine kept going. "That's only going to work once," he said.

"Make haste to the vault," Artemis said. "We'll be safe inside."

Oliver hit the exit ramp at top speed and had to brake sharply to make the turn toward *Casa de Flores*. He remembered the route well enough. The cyborgs would have no way to anticipate where they were going, so roadblocks shouldn't be a concern here, unless the helicopter overhead was able to coordinate with the five Humvees now chasing them to start cutting streets off. Hopefully they'd be quick enough for that not to be a concern.

Oliver kept the Humvee's speed up as he entered the former retirement community, driving over what remained of the front gate, which was now just a piece of twisted, charred metal. Oliver stared, amazed at the destruction laid out in front of them. Whatever defenses *Casa de Flores* had had, they'd been used to full effect when the cyborgs had invaded. Several of the houses had been razed and several had clearly never been occupied in the first place; they appeared to have been covers for stationary weapons platforms, instead. Oliver could easily make out the remains of three gun turrets that looked like something straight out of a video game. The shell of a burned-out tank sat in the middle of one street, and another had been blown to pieces. It appeared to have taken a bomb hit from directly overhead. "They put up one hell of a fight," Tyler marveled.

"That was their purpose," Artemis said. "Stop in front of the last house. You remember which one, Oliver?"

Oliver did. That house remained untouched, although the front door had been left open. The cyborgs had probably gone inside to look for people and left after finding none. They wouldn't have known about the closet's secret function, of course. Oliver pulled into the driveway and they climbed out. In the distance he heard the screeching of tires. The cyborgs weren't far behind, and the helicopter that had dogged them for the last twenty miles was directly overhead. It had been joined by another, Oliver noted. It hardly mattered now, though. They were here.

The three of them hurried inside the house, Tyler bringing

the picnic basket along, and headed for the closet. Once inside, Artemis shut the doors behind them and said, "Identify." The closet lit up around them as the scanner activated, stopping at each of their eye levels, before dropping to their feet and rising again. "Artemis. Alpha One access." The closet chimed.

Tyler cleared his throat. "Tyler Jacobsen. Alpha access." The closet chimed again.

"Oliver Jones. Alpha access," Oliver said, just as he had the last time he'd been here. This time there was no chime. He heard the front door crash open as the cyborgs stormed inside.

"What's wrong?" Oliver asked.

"Seven never authorized you in this timeline," Artemis said. "I should have remembered that." She sighed. "Artemis. Alpha One access. Emergency protocol three." She looked at each of them in turn. "Now this really is a one-way trip."

"What do you mean?" Oliver asked. Then he heard several loud bangs and a sound like metal tearing, and the elevator went into freefall.

"Is that supposed to happen?" Tyler shouted as they fell.

"You did hear me say *emergency*?" Artemis asked him.

Metal screeched as emergency brakes slammed into operation and the elevator began to slow down. Far above them Oliver heard more explosions. "What's happening up there?"

"I would think none of you know the meaning of the word *emergency*," Artemis noted. "The house above us is being demolished. When that process is complete, the shaft we currently occupy will be collapsed. If the cyborgs ever manage to find it, it will take them months to dig down to us. The matter should no longer be relevant at that time."

Shortly the elevator ground to a halt and the doors slid open. The vault was exactly as Oliver remembered it. Above them he heard a final explosion, and then everything was quiet.

Artemis stepped forward as Oliver heard the humming of a new electronic system powering up. Pinpoints of red light appeared, sweeping across the floor in front of her. "What is that?" Oliver asked.

"Targeting system," Tyler said. "You're an intruder."

"Artemis. Alpha One access. Disable internal security," the girl said. The pinpoints of light disappeared.

"Was that for the turrets?" Oliver asked.

"Yes," Artemis said. "They will recognize you as hostile, so I cannot leave them active. Oliver, please go and check on the mirror." She looked around. "I have a few items I must collect before we leave. We will meet you at the time machine."

"Does it matter if the mirror is still there?" Oliver asked. "We're going back in time, after all."

Artemis stared at him. "Go and check on the mirror," she said firmly.

"Fine, fine." Oliver started down one of the aisles. He was fairly certain he knew where he was going.

"I still can't believe we have a time machine," he heard Tyler say as they started off in another direction. "What are we picking up, anyway?"

Oliver found the mirror without any trouble. It was no longer broken, and he could see his own reflection clearly. The tape that had formerly protected it was gone, though. He supposed if the mirror had never been broken, the tape never would have been put up in the first place. It seemed strange to him that the mirror looked so ordinary. He'd never have suspected it was anything other than what it looked like.

His seemingly pointless assignment complete, he turned and started for the time machine, reaching it just moments after Tyler and Artemis. Tyler swung the hatch open and helped Artemis inside, then turned to pick up the picnic basket.

"What were you looking for?" Oliver asked.

Tyler looked away. "Just stuff we need for later."

"What stuff?"

"Gentlemen," Artemis's voice called from inside. "While time may no longer seem like a factor to you, I assure you it is to me. Come along. Now."

Tyler climbed into the time machine, with Oliver following a moment later. He pulled the hatch shut behind them.

All things considered, Oliver wasn't sure what he'd have expected the inside of a time machine to look like. Lots of lights and futuristic design, maybe. Instead, it was nothing spectacular. There was a cockpit in the forward part that reminded him of an old airplane. Two wooden benches lined the narrow passenger area with an open space between them. It would have been spacious enough to hold maybe eight people, if needed, but with its low ceilings and lack of interior lighting felt cramped. Dust covered everything. Oliver doubted it had been cleaned since its first use in the 1940's, if it ever had been cleaned at all.

Artemis took a seat at the controls and began flicking switches. A row of interior lights came on, albeit dimly, and several instruments in front of her lit up. "You know how to drive this thing?" Oliver asked.

"I read the manual some time ago," she replied. "I remember enough."

Oliver took a look at the cockpit. The few things that were labeled were in German. He wouldn't have been able to make heads or tails of it. "Did Sally speak German?"

"It is not particularly complex," Artemis said. "She wouldn't have needed much, and clearly she had been planning what she was going to do." She studied the console. "She entered a date that would have given her ample time to accomplish her mission, but I should warn you it is very unlikely we will emerge at the same time."

"Why not?" Tyler asked. "If we use the same settings she did, shouldn't we get there right when she does?"

"Time travel is not an exact science," Artemis said. "If it were easy, everyone would do it. The date is more of a suggestion than an explicit instruction. We may arrive when she does, or a day or two before or after. We will know soon enough." She ran her hands over the controls and looked back at Tyler and Oliver. "You may want to hang on to something."

Oliver looked around. "There really isn't much back here."

Artemis shrugged. "Oh, well." She turned a lever and a humming noise began reverberating through the vessel's hull as what sounded like a rocket engine began powering up. "I am engaging the system now." She flipped another switch, hesitated for one small moment, and then pressed a series of buttons.

The time machine began vibrating as if it were being shaken

from the outside. Oliver looked out through one of the portholes. Nothing appeared to be changing. Then again, they were only going back about a year. He had no idea how long it had been since the vault had been redecorated, or if anything in this wing had been moved around recently. "Shut your eyes," Artemis said.

Oliver shut his eyes, but it wasn't enough to block out the intense flash of light that came next. When he opened his eyes again he found himself seeing stars. The time machine had gone silent. Oliver looked through the porthole again but still saw nothing new. "Are we here?"

"We are here, Mr. Jones. The hatch please, Mr. Jacobsen." Tyler turned the wheel that secured the hatch, pushed it open, and looked outside.

"It looks exactly the same," he said.

"So it should. I will disembark first. The turrets will need to be deactivated again. You two should take this opportunity to change into your normal clothes. You look ridiculous."

"You said we looked like cyborgs," Oliver protested.

"Yes, I did. I did not say it was a good look." She stepped outside and Oliver heard her addressing the security system again.

Oliver and Tyler stripped off their cyborg armor and got dressed, then joined Artemis outside the time machine. "You have the basket?" she asked Tyler. He held it up to show her. "Good. Let us go to the mirror. Follow me." She led them back the way Oliver had just come from, although that had been over a year in the future. The concept was a little difficult to wrap his head around.

The mirror stood exactly where he had left it. "So how do we…" Oliver began. Artemis did not wait for him to finish the question. She didn't stop walking, but just stepped forward and into the mirror, vanishing before Oliver's eyes as if she'd stepped through a wall of opaque water. The glass appeared to ripple slightly as she passed through, and then resumed its solid appearance.

"Yeah, I never really got used to that," Tyler said. "Don't worry. It doesn't hurt." He stepped up and walked through the mirror, disappearing just as Artemis had. Oliver was alone in the vault.

He hesitated for a moment, then stepped closer to the mirror. He reached out slowly and touched his reflection with his index finger, watching as it vanished through the glass, and then pulled it back again. His finger tingled just a bit, but he felt unharmed. Oliver took a deep breath. Putting an arm over his eyes to shield them, he stepped through the mirror.

The sensation of walking through the glass was unlike anything he had yet experienced. He felt a cool wind that made his skin tingle, and had a sensation as if he'd been picked up by a gust of wind and pushed forward a few steps before being placed back down on the ground. His eyes saw nothing but white light, but he couldn't help but shut them. When he opened them again he found he was standing in what appeared to have once been a large airplane hangar. The room was about half the size of a football field with a high, curved ceiling. He, Artemis, and Tyler were standing at the top of a metal ramp with a mirror that appeared identical to the one in their vault just behind them. In front of them stood two automated machine gun turrets pointed directly at them. Half a dozen soldiers in camouflage fatigues stood between the turrets, each holding an assault rifle with the barrels pointed at the ground.

An older man wearing a black beret stepped through a door off to the side and hurried forward. "Forgive me, Madam President," he said. "We had no idea you were inbound, or we would have prepared a proper reception for you. I'll have one of my men get a pot of tea started for you and your associates."

"Madam President?" Oliver whispered to Tyler.

"Just go with it," Tyler whispered back.

Artemis walked down the ramp. "It is no matter, Lieutenant Forrest. I apologize that our coming was not announced, but we have urgent business here. Where is Colonel Rain?"

"She is…" Lieutenant Forrest frowned. "This is a bit strange."

"Quickly, Lieutenant. When did you see her last?"

"She came through the portal last week, but the strange thing was we didn't realize she had ever left. I'd thought she was at Federation Command."

"Did you challenge her?"

"Of course, but she was in dress uniform and she passed the bio scan. There was no question it was her, so I assumed someone had forgotten to make a log entry. She took a weapon from the armory and went on her way."

"Did she say where she was going?"

"No, and I didn't ask."

"They're as scared of her here as we are back home," Tyler whispered.

"That's not really a surprise," Oliver whispered back.

"You say she was here last week?" Artemis asked. "It seems more time has passed than I expected."

"Madam President?" Forrest asked.

"Nothing," she said. "What is the situation on the ground?"

Forrest bit his lip. "Federation City stands, but..."

"Be frank, Lieutenant."

"We're losing, Madam President. If I can be frank, we're losing. The cyborgs are shelling the outer areas of the city and their infantry is advancing too quickly for us. Some at Command think we'll last another month. Others think that's too optimistic. But thanks to your wise counsel, I'm sure that won't be the case." He frowned slightly. "Come to think of it, I thought you were *also* at Federation Command..."

"Clearly I am not," Artemis said. "You should review your log keeping procedures so as not to make such mistakes in the future."

"Of course. I apologize, Madam President."

"Calm yourself, Lieutenant. I believe we yet have cause for hope. But for now, I will require you to provide a conveyance that can carry myself and my trusted advisors."

"Trusted advisors?" Oliver whispered.

"Of course," Lieutenant Forrest said. "I will have an escort assembled at once..."

"That will not be necessary. My advisors are more than capable of escorting me, and your good work is needed here. This location must be held, Lieutenant. You need only provide a vehicle so I may join Colonel Rain at Federation Command."

Forrest nodded at one of his soldiers, who rushed for the door. "It will be done immediately, Madam President."

Chapter 18

"Madam President?" Oliver repeated. They were in a military sedan Lieutenant Forrest had procured for them. Tyler drove with Artemis sitting next to him, picnic basket on her lap. Oliver had taken a seat in the rear. Artemis had not yet chosen a destination for them, merely telling Tyler to "drive around" for the time being.

"You can thank Sally for that," Artemis said. "It is how she introduced me when I accompanied her here through the mirror the first time. I believe she thought it was funny."

Oliver didn't normally think of Sally as having a sense of humor. "How did you sell that to everyone else?"

"I did not. I merely performed one of my many miracles for them."

"You found a coin behind somebody's ear?"

"No. I walked through a mirror. To the uninitiated, it is a fairly impressive feat."

Oliver would have had to admit that it was. "So what do we do next?"

"I am considering that matter. I am waiting for a memory."

"You're waiting for *what*?"

"Time travel is a strange thing, Mr. Jones, particularly for me. In this case, Tyler and I both exist in this world in other places. I am already aware of my other self. I can feel it, on the edge of my consciousness. No doubt she is aware of me, as well. I fear this experience will shortly grow very unpleasant."

"I don't feel anything," Tyler said.

"You are not me. There should never be two of me in the same place at the same time." Artemis massaged the bridge of her nose. "Keep driving."

"Can I get one of those muffins?" Tyler asked. Artemis fished one out of the picnic basket and handed it to him.

"You shouldn't eat and drive," Oliver said.

"You think anyone is going to give me a ticket? We've got the President here."

Tyler kept the car in motion and Oliver took the time to look out at the city. Artemis had said that it would be very similar to his own world, but Oliver had spotted nothing that stood out as very strange so far. Federation City looked much like every other large city he'd ever visited. As they drove they passed convenience stores and restaurants, small office complexes and parking lots. From their location he could see what had to be the downtown area in the distance, where skyscrapers seemed to compete with each other to see which could reach the highest. Beyond them black smoke rose into the sky.

"That doesn't look like a normal fire," Oliver said.

Tyler looked out the window. "I'm not sure exactly *when* we are, to tell you the truth. The last time I was here, before the cure, the cyborgs were bombing some of the outer areas. That's probably what that is."

"Indeed," Artemis said.

"Well, other than that, it seems pretty ordinary here," Oliver said. "This place is just like home." He'd barely finished the sentence when he spotted an airship overhead. It reminded him of the blimps that flew over stadiums during sporting events, but this one was reinforced with steel plates that wrapped around it from top to bottom. The crew area underneath was larger, ran from one end of the airship to the other, and had missile launchers jutting out from the sides.

"Forget it," Oliver said.

Artemis sighed. "Linnea has gone missing," she said. Her voice sounded pained.

"What?" Tyler asked. "How do you know that?"

"My memories are beginning to merge with those of the me that exists here."

"Oh."

"Are you all right?" Oliver asked.

"No," Artemis said. "It is quite painful."

"Can I help?"

"Thank you, Mr. Jones, but no. Tyler, stop at one of the convenience stores. I need some aspirin."

"Will that help?" Oliver asked.

"It cannot hurt."

Tyler parked in front of a small shop. "I don't have any of their money," he said.

Artemis went back into the picnic basket and came out with a few purple bills. "That will be more than enough. Get some water, also. Attempt not to buy any junk food."

Tyler disappeared inside the store. "Mr. Jones, should I lose consciousness at any time, wake me at once. Do not let me sleep."

"Is there any reason why not?"

"Yes."

Oliver waited but Artemis didn't say anything else until Tyler came back outside and handed her a bottle of aspirin. She took two of the pills and washed them down with water while Tyler handed another bottle back to Oliver.

"Thanks," Oliver said.

"You don't look so good," Tyler said to Artemis.

"I'm fine, Mr. Jacobsen, but I may need you to drive me somewhere shortly," Artemis said. "Go outside and find a car, and wait for me unless I call you back here."

Tyler cast a worried look at Oliver in the rear view mirror. "Um...we're already in a car."

Artemis blinked. "Oh. I apologize, Mr. Jacobsen. That was not me. That is, it was the *other* me. She is at Federation Command and is now well aware of the time fracture. She will be attempting to decide how to proceed."

"Okay," Tyler said. "Is there one of those magic time

houses here?"

"Not that I am aware of, and hence not that she is aware of." She looked at the radio unit in the car's dashboard. "Call Federation Command on the executive frequency."

Tyler fiddled with the console for a moment. "I barely remember how this thing works," he said.

"Oh, for goodness sake," Artemis said. She turned a knob on the console and pressed a switch. "Federation Command, this is President Artemis speaking."

Static crackled on the speaker for a moment. "Federation Command," a man's voice said.

"I will speak with Colonel Rain. I believe she is in the operations center at this moment."

"Colonel Rain is occupied with a personal matter," the voice said.

"That is not my concern," Artemis snapped. "I will speak with her immediately."

There was a short pause. "Forgive me, Madam President, but...aren't you in the building? I thought I saw you on your way to the operations center just a minute ago."

"Clearly you did not. I will ask you not to waste my time any further."

"My apologies, Madam President. I'll put you through now."

A longer pause followed, and then Sally's voice came over the speaker. "Artemis? Where are you? Did you find anything on my sister?"

Artemis nodded to herself. "I have not, Salera, but I am endeavoring to do so at this very moment. Could you please remind me of the last time you saw Linnea?"

"You want to go over that again?"

"Please humor me. Time is a critical factor."

"Yeah, I figured that, so I don't know why we're...oh, forget it. I haven't actually *seen* her in months. I visited her at the Kholon facility after I got back from St. Louis, but we've been kind of busy since then."

"And when did she disappear?"

"*When*? Artemis, you know I love you, but I swear to the gods you're trying my fucking patience right now."

"Please, Sally."

"Sally?"

"Salera. I'm sorry. When did she disappear?"

Sally sighed. "A week ago. She walked out of the Kholon facility without a word to anyone and nobody's seen her since. Nobody. But you know this already. I don't know why you're asking me."

"I see," Artemis said. "Let us consider a question I won't have asked you before. If you had taken her somewhere, where would you have gone?"

"If *I* had taken her somewhere? What the hell kind of question..." her voice trailed off. "Here's a question," she said. "Who the hell are you?"

"It's me, Salera. Artemis. You know my voice."

"No, you're not Artemis, because Artemis just walked into

the operations center and I'm looking at her right now. Who are you?"

"An excellent question," Artemis's voice came over the speaker. "Who is speaking?"

"This just got weird," Oliver said quietly.

"I think it was pretty weird before," Tyler whispered.

Artemis hesitated for a moment, then said two words in a language Oliver didn't understand. She clicked the radio off. "Drive us to a public place," she said to Tyler. "That park where they sell those sausage rolls you like should do very nicely."

"I'm not going to argue with that," Tyler said. "I missed those." He turned the ignition and pulled the car out of the parking lot.

"What did you say to her?" Oliver asked. "I mean, to yourself."

"I told her to find me," Artemis said.

Chapter 19

Half an hour later they sat next to a large fountain in an open-air park adjacent to a shopping mall. Hundreds of people walked all around them drinking coffee, shopping, and chatting as if they didn't have a care in the world. If Oliver hadn't known better, he'd have guessed that none of them knew the outskirts of their city were burning.

Oliver wondered for a moment if the conversation with Sally meant they were fugitives now, but decided against it. Sally would have had no reason to think she was actually speaking with another version of Artemis. She may have taken it as a very strange prank call, but even if it had been reported, nobody would know who to be searching for. Nobody except the other Artemis, that was.

Tyler was halfway through his third sausage roll. "So how are you going to find us?" he asked between bites. "Or how are you going to find *you*, I guess. Time travel gives me a headache."

"That is a normal side effect," Artemis said.

"Oh," Tyler said. "I was just using it as a figure of speech, actually. I don't really have a headache."

"Then you are indeed fortunate. Mine is getting worse. I do not expect it to improve until we leave this place."

Oliver didn't have a headache, either, but he also didn't have another version of himself running around the city. "Do you feel *anything* weird?" he asked Tyler.

"Nope. I mean, I guess there's some déjà vu. I never expected to see this place again after Sally smashed the mirror."

Oliver didn't think that really counted as déjà vu, but he didn't see the need to correct him. "So how will you find us?" he asked Artemis.

Artemis nodded at a nearby security camera. "I have been gazing at that camera since we arrived."

"Great," Oliver said. "And that is going to help us…how? Are we planning on robbing someone?"

"No, Mr. Jones. My other self will have known I was not an impostor. Even if I could not recognize my own voice over the speaker, there is likely nobody else in the universe who speaks my first language." She glanced at Oliver. "Before you bother to ask, it does not have a name. It did not need one, back then."

"How long will it take?" Tyler asked.

"I will have instructed Seven to check the security feeds. I would think…" she trailed off as a sedan marked with military insignia pulled up and parked a dozen feet away from them. "Well, I thought it might take a little longer than *that*."

Oliver watched as the rear door of the car opened and another Artemis stepped out. To his surprise, she wore a dark blue military uniform with gold patches on the arms and a large number of ribbons pinned to the front. "Did you actually join their army?" he asked.

"No, of course not. It was a ceremonial uniform. Sally asked me to wear it as a show of solidarity." Artemis sighed. "She said I would be a beacon of hope for her people."

"Sally used the words *beacon of hope*?" Tyler asked. "Really?"

"She did." She gave Oliver another look. "She was not always the person you know, Mr. Jones. Do endeavor to remember that."

Oliver wasn't sure why that comment had been directed at him, but it didn't seem like something worth arguing about, particularly when the second version of Artemis was approaching their position.

The uniformed Artemis stopped directly in front of her counterpart. "It appears we have a serious problem," she said.

"We do," Artemis said. "We are aware of Linnea Rain's disappearance."

"Our presence here suggests the foreshock we felt here a week ago was in fact that of a timequake."

"We are correct in that assessment. The timeline has been corrupted."

"This is getting a little confusing," Oliver said. "Can we call one of you *Artemis One* and one of you *Artemis Two*?"

"No," they said in unison.

"Fine," Oliver said. "I'll just shut up now."

"It is imperative that we locate Sally Rain," Oliver's Artemis said.

"It is unlikely that we are referring to Colonel Rain, who is in the command center at this very moment."

"We are not. We are referring to Sally Rain, who took the time machine in Vault 3 without authorization and attempted to change what happened here."

The uniformed Artemis was silent for a moment. "We appear to have failed to help these people, then."

"We have failed in many things," Oliver's Artemis said. "While we may reflect on them later, we have only a short time in which to act."

"Our headache grows worse," the uniformed Artemis said. "Even now we are beginning to have trouble differentiating ourselves."

"Indeed." Oliver's Artemis opened the picnic basket and removed an automatic syringe. "Tell Seven to inject Colonel Rain with this. We may tell her it is some manner of vaccine against cyborg conversion."

"We find it unlikely she will believe that."

Oliver's Artemis shook her head. "Then tell her whatever we feel is necessary. She trusts us. She is not likely to object."

The uniformed Artemis took the syringe. "Ah, yes," she said, examining the device. "We have not seen this for quite some time."

"It has limited applications," Oliver's Artemis said. "This is one of them."

"We are betraying her."

"We regret that. However, if we cannot locate her quickly, two timelines will be corrupted beyond repair."

"What is that?" Oliver asked. "Poison? You're not going to kill her?"

"No, Mr. Jones," Oliver's Artemis said. "It is a radioactive isotope with a very long half-life. It will enable us to locate her, and nothing more."

"Inject her in the past and the future Sally turns radioactive," Tyler said. "Smart." He frowned. "I think. So the radioactive Sally goes through the portal and..." he thought it over. "Forget it. I don't even care at this point."

"That will do, Mr. Jacobsen," Oliver's Artemis said.

The uniformed Artemis nodded. "Very well. We will address this matter shortly." She glanced at Oliver. "We did not expect to see this one here."

"We will speak no more on that subject," Oliver's Artemis said. "The matter remains unresolved."

"Very well."

"Wait," Oliver said. "What did you mean you didn't expect to see me?"

"How many meanings can that statement have?" the uniformed Artemis asked. She looked back at her future self. "How will we know if we have succeeded?"

"If we do not meet again in this world. If we do..." she shrugged. "We have no further solutions, and all will be lost."

The uniformed Artemis turned and walked back to her car. Oliver watched as it drove away. "Was that you in there driving?" he asked Tyler.

"I don't know," Tyler said. "I don't remember it."

"What did she mean?" Oliver asked Artemis. "You didn't expect to see me?"

"Mr. Jones, forgive me for my directness, but I am in a great deal of pain. So…shut up. Surely we have more important things to concern ourselves with right now."

"Will you tell me later?"

Artemis considered that. "Probably not."

Oliver cursed under his breath. "What do we do now?" Tyler asked.

Artemis removed one of Seven's tablet computers from the picnic basket and turned it on. "We wait," she said. "It will not take long."

Chapter 20

Not long turned out to be about twenty minutes, during which time Artemis entertained no further questions from either Oliver or Tyler. The girl spent most of the time massaging her temples with her fingers. At one point Tyler asked if she wanted him to run out to find something stronger than aspirin for her to take. "It will not matter," she said. "The discomfort will continue until I no longer exist in two places at once." She glanced at the tablet computer on her lap. It displayed a wireframe map of the city, but nothing more.

"What exactly are we waiting for?" Oliver asked. He barely had the question out before two red dots appeared on the screen. Artemis studied them for a moment, then manipulated the touchscreen to zoom in on one.

"What's that?" Tyler asked.

"It is Sally's location."

"Why are there two of them?" Oliver asked. "Oh, I get it. One of them is the past her, and the other is the her we're looking for?"

"How fortunate that we saved you from the cyborgs," Artemis said. "Who else would be here to point out the obvious to me if we had not?"

Oliver blinked in surprise. "Um…okay."

Artemis shook her head. "I apologize, Mr. Jones. I am not feeling myself at the moment." She tapped the screen. "You were correct in your assessment. This is Sally's location."

"Where is it?" Tyler asked.

"It is exactly where she would never think to look," Artemis said. She sighed. "I could probably have guessed it myself, if I was able to think clearly."

"Where?" Oliver asked.

"It is the house where she and her sister grew up."

"They don't visit their parents much?"

"Their parents are long dead," Artemis said. "But that is not the point. They did not have a happy childhood. Sally hates that house more than…more than anything, I should imagine." Artemis watched for a moment as another airship passed by overhead. "We will be needing the car, Mr. Jacobsen."

The Rain house was in the suburbs on the outskirts of the city, closer to the combat area than Oliver would have liked. The black smoke that he'd seen rising in the distance before was now uncomfortably close, although he knew it was still many miles from their position. Every now and then he saw military jets overhead, patrolling in groups of four. There didn't seem to be any imminent danger, but he hoped this wouldn't be a lengthy visit. Lieutenant Forrest hadn't been exaggerating back at the hanger where they'd crossed into this world. The war really wasn't going well.

"Should we be armed for this?" Tyler asked. "I doubt Sally is going to be happy to see us."

"There is little point to that," Artemis noted. "Even if you were willing to shoot her, which I know you are not, do you think you could outdraw her?"

"Of course not."

"She shouldn't be expecting us," Oliver said. "She doesn't know what happened back on our Earth."

"She will know the moment she sees us," Artemis said. "I do not expect her to take it well. While I doubt there will be a physical confrontation, you should both prepare yourselves to attempt to restrain her. Your werewolf strength may be needed, Mr. Jacobsen."

"I doubt it would make any difference," Tyler said.

"She's really that good?" Oliver asked.

"You've seen her fight," Tyler said. "She'd wipe the floor with me no matter what form I was in. I'd put money on her over pretty much anyone, except maybe Maria. That was another reason we wanted her with us."

Oliver recalled seeing what the vampire had done to a room full of cyborgs. He wondered what it would have been like if she and Sally had come to blows. Regardless of who won, the collateral damage would probably have been fairly impressive.

Artemis pointed to a small, two-story house with a "for sale" sign on the front yard. The house and the entire neighborhood appeared abandoned. Oliver hadn't seen a single person outside and nearly every house on this block had its windows boarded up. The proximity to the war front had probably driven most of the people here away, he thought. Nobody wanted to be home when the cyborgs came marching through backyards, converting everyone they could get their hands on and shooting everyone else. Oliver found it hard to blame them. He wondered where the refugees had gone, not that the answer would have meant much to him. This world was similar to his own in many ways, but he had no idea exactly what territory the American Federation encompassed, or how much of it had been conquered.

Tyler pulled the car up to the front of the house and killed the engine. "I really don't want to be doing this."

"We can't have everything we want in life," Artemis snapped. "I know I certainly haven't." She stepped out of the car and slammed the door shut behind her.

"What was that?" Oliver asked.

"Her head is really messing with her," Tyler said. "I've never seen her like this."

"Is there something we can do?"

Tyler sighed. "I don't understand what's going on with her," he said, "but I know there's something strange about how she interacts with time." He watched as the girl started up the steps to the house. "I don't think it's so much that she's lived a long time. I think time just forgot about her at some point, and being here, it's remembering her."

"That doesn't make a lot of sense," Oliver said.

"I just told you I don't understand it," Tyler said. "You know what my job here is? I eat too much, I geek out over aliens, and I turn into a big-ass wolf when somebody needs to get smacked around. This shit is way above my pay grade."

Oliver stared at him. "Are *you* all right?"

"No," Tyler said. "I don't want to be here right now. I would rather fight the whole damn cyborg army by myself than walk in there and tell Sally her sister has to die."

"Wait...*that's* what we're doing?" Oliver didn't recall hearing this part of the plan, but then again, he wasn't exactly sure what their plan was supposed to have been.

"Why the hell do you think we're here?" Tyler asked. He got out of the car.

Oliver followed him a moment later and they joined Artemis at the front door. Artemis rang the doorbell. A minute passed with no response. Oliver took a step back and looked at the house. All of the blinds were shut, and he couldn't see anything that looked like someone peeking out at them. "You sure she's here?" he asked.

"Quite sure, Mr. Jones." She rang the bell again. "Open the door, Salera!"

After another moment the door slowly opened. Sally Rain stood there in camouflage pants and a white tank top, looking as if she'd neither slept nor bathed in quite some time. She looked at the three of them in turn, finally turning to Artemis with a sigh. "Damn it," she said quietly. "It didn't work."

"Might we come in, Salera?" Artemis asked.

Sally stepped aside and Artemis brushed past her into the house. "Hi," Oliver said.

"Hi." She gave him a small smile. "Hey there, T."

Tyler shoved his hands into his pockets and went inside the house. After a moment, Oliver followed him. Sally closed the door behind them.

The front door led straight into the house's living room. There was little furniture other than an old couch, a dusty coffee table, and a few mismatched chairs that looked like they'd been collected from other rooms. A military radio unit sat on the coffee table, squawking every now and again with chatter. Next to it sat a holstered pistol. Oliver wasn't particularly surprised that a house for sale in a neighborhood where nobody wanted to live didn't exactly look like a home. Nor was he surprised to see a red-haired woman with her right wrist handcuffed to one of the chairs. She wore a blue lab coat and also looked as if she hadn't been sleeping much lately, or at least not sleeping very well.

"Artemis," the woman said. "I can't say I'm surprised to see you here."

"Hello, Linnea. It is refreshing to see you again, although I regret these circumstances. You already know Mr. Jacobsen," she said, nodding at Tyler. "This other gentleman is our associate, Mr. Jones." She took a seat near Linnea across from the couch. Tyler sat down next to her.

"Oliver," he introduced himself, looking into Linnea's emerald eyes. The family resemblance was striking. Linnea could nearly have been Sally's twin, except that she was at least five years younger and somehow didn't seem to have the edge that Sally did. Sally was a lioness always ready to pounce. Linnea was a lioness who had better things to do with her time.

Sally took a seat on the couch. "There's food in the kitchen," she said to Tyler. "It's all convenience store stuff I picked up. Nothing good."

"We had sausage rolls," Tyler said, not looking at her.

"*You* had sausage rolls," Oliver noted.

Sally smiled faintly. "You always did like those." She sighed. "So," she said to Artemis. "What went wrong?"

"Might you release your sister from confinement before we speak? She looks quite uncomfortable."

Linnea rattled the handcuffs binding her to the chair. "That would be nice."

Sally looked her sister in the eyes. "Only if you promise not to try to run away again. I don't want to hurt you."

Linnea rattled the handcuffs again. "I'm not entertaining the idea I could get past you," she glanced at Artemis briefly. "At least not while you're conscious. Take these damn things off me."

Sally stood up, crossed over to where her sister sat, and uncuffed her. Linnea rubbed her wrist with her left hand. "Thank you."

"Please sit down," Artemis said. Sally took her seat on the couch again. "I will not pretend I do not understand your motivations here, Salera…"

"Don't call me that," Sally said. "Only my sister gets to use that name."

"Very well." Artemis looked at Linnea. "What did she tell you?"

"Everything," Linnea said. "I can't say I believed any of it, at first. I thought she'd finally lost her mind. And then I heard her voice on that radio saying I'd gone missing, when I was sitting right here with her." She shook her head. "Time travel. I had enough trouble believing you were from another world, until I saw you walk through that mirror with my own eyes. I'm not sure why I was so surprised you had a time machine, too."

Artemis nodded. "And I'm not sure why I was so surprised your sister used it to try to save you. Well, tea seems in order. Do you have any?"

"There's some in the kitchen," Sally said. "I think you got me hooked on the stuff. I missed it when I got over here."

Artemis nodded at Tyler, who disappeared into the kitchen. Oliver, who hadn't been entirely sure what to do with himself up until this point, took one of the empty chairs. "You tricked me," he said to Sally.

"Yeah." Sally looked away. "I'm…I'm sorry about that, Oliver. I really am. I would have just asked you to help me, but…"

"You thought I wouldn't?"

"No. I know you would have. You're that kind of guy. But you said you had to believe." She shook her head. "You said you had to believe, so I told you the time machine worked. I hid its number tag in the warehouse so you couldn't look it up and see that it didn't."

Oliver nodded. "I'd sort of guessed that. It seemed weird that everything else was in place but that one number was nowhere to be found."

"It was an ambitious plan, Sally," Artemis said. "I won't deny that. How did you imagine it would succeed?"

"The Kholon facility should have been bombed yesterday," Sally said. "It wasn't. I must have gotten the timing wrong. We just have to wait now. They're so close to the cure, as soon as they finish it…"

"*I'm* close to the cure, Sal," Linnea said. "Me. I don't want to sound arrogant here, but…" she glanced at Artemis. "I guess this isn't the place for false modesty, is it?"

"It is not."

"My research is years ahead of everybody else's." Linnea left her chair and went to sit next to Sally on the couch. "Even if the rest of my team understood my notes, which they don't, they wouldn't know where to start with it. Hell, I wasn't even sure it would work, myself. Now that I know it does, I could finish it in a few hours."

Sally nodded. Oliver saw tears starting to form in her eyes. "Then they just need to get to work," she said. "Radio them and tell them what to do."

"You're asking me to explain algebra to a monkey. Over the phone." Linnea shook her head. "It has to be me."

"Sally?" Oliver asked. "Look, I'm sorry, but this plan…it didn't work. You lost."

Linnea looked at Artemis. "You wouldn't be here if we'd won the war," she said. "How bad was it?"

"This planet was conquered," Artemis said. "I would expect that, two months from now, there will not be a single unconverted human left alive."

"*Gods,*" Linnea whispered. "I knew we were losing, but…" she shook her head. "I still had some hope."

"Unfortunately, you were the hope, Linnea, and your sister has removed you from the equation. In the correct timeline, you cured the cyborg contagion and saved the world. And, in effect, my own." Artemis looked at Sally. "When the cyborgs finished conquering this world, they used their teleportation technology to invade ours. Their victory is assured there, as well. It is only a matter of time."

Sally wrung her hands together. "There has to be another way."

"How long has it been since you slept?" Oliver asked.

"A while." She nodded at Linnea. "This one keeps yelling at me."

"You tricked me into coming out here and handcuffed me to a chair."

"You kept trying to run away!"

"Imagine that!"

"Enough," Artemis said. She rubbed her temples as Tyler returned from the kitchen with two Styrofoam cups full of tea. He sat them down on the table and headed back for more. Artemis picked up her cup, sniffed it, and made a face. "I suppose this will have to do."

"It was all they had at the store," Sally said.

Artemis sipped the tea and put her cup back down. "It is time we end this, Sally."

"I'm not letting her go until after the bombing," Sally said. "She can go somewhere else and finish her work then."

"I'd have to start over. Everything I have is at Kholon," Linnea said. "The war will be over by the time I'm done."

"Then somebody else can do it."

"We just went over this," Linnea sighed. "Do you really think if anyone else could do it I wouldn't be on that radio right now?" She looked at Artemis. "Maybe since I know there's an attack coming, there's a chance? I don't need long to make it work. I could get in and get out, or at least evacuate the others."

"The weapon," Sally said. "Use the weapon, instead. You finished that."

Linnea's eyes widened slightly. "How do you even know about that thing?"

"It was..."

"Your code was discovered at a later time," Artemis interrupted. "After the cure was deployed."

Linnea took a deep breath. "Well, thank god for that. I was never going to release it, not unless it was the last thing standing between the human race and extinction. It's monstrous, Sal. It doesn't just shut down the A.I.; it kills the bots and the hosts die. There's no way to bring them back."

"So what?" Sally asked. "You'll live. The cyborgs will be dead. The other world never gets invaded. We win." She looked at Artemis. "Would that satisfy you?"

"Do you think this is about my satisfaction?" Artemis asked. "I assure you, regardless of what happens next, I will not be satisfied in any sense of the word."

Linnea took her sister by the shoulder. "Look at me, Sal. There are twenty million cyborgs out there. Do you really think I'd murder all of them just to save my own skin? Really?"

"They aren't people anymore," Sally said. "They're robots."

"They're really not," Linnea shook her head. "They're just lost."

Sally grimaced. "You can't make her go," she said to Artemis. "I won't let you."

"I have no intention of making her do anything," Artemis said. "I have only advised you of the facts of the situation. You may do as you please, Linnea, but I suspect you have already made your decision." Artemis went back to drinking her horrible tea. Tyler returned to the room with two more Styrofoam cups, handing one to Oliver and putting the other down in front of Linnea. Oliver sipped his tea. He had never been much of a tea drinker before he'd met Artemis and didn't have much of a palate for it, but even he knew what was in his cup was awful. Tyler took a seat next to Artemis and waited.

"You're not leaving," Sally said to Linnea. "I don't care. I'll let the world burn before I lose you again."

Linnea sighed. "Those really are the only two choices here, aren't they? You really would, wouldn't you? Let our world burn?"

"Of course I would. You're my sister."

"Okay. You win. We don't have to talk about this anymore." Linnea slid closer to her sister on the couch and put her arms around her. Oliver saw her make eye contact with Artemis. Artemis nodded ever so slightly.

Linnea stroked Sally's back for a moment and then pulled away. "Drink your tea," she said. "I have some other things to say to you."

Sally took her cup and sipped it. "This really *is* bad." She laughed. "I could never make it like yours," she said to Artemis.

"It does help to purchase a higher quality of product," Artemis noted. "I doubt you would find anything suitable for human consumption at a convenience store."

"It's got caffeine," Sally said. "I think it's all that's been keeping me awake the last few days."

Linnea watched as Sally drank her tea, then took the cup out of her hand and put it down on the table. "Look at me, okay? I love you so much, Sal," she said.

"I love you, too."

Linnea smiled wistfully. "You were my hero when we were little. I want you to know that. You still are. You'll always be my hero."

"Hey," Sally said, patting her sister on the arm. She reached for her cup. "Why are you talking like that? It'll be okay. I'll talk to Federation Command. If they know what I know…" she looked at Tyler and frowned. "Why are you crying?"

Oliver looked over at Tyler, surprised to see that tears were streaming down his friend's face.

"Tyler?" Sally asked. "What's…" the Styrofoam cup dropped from her hand, bouncing once on the couch and spilling the last of its contents everywhere.

"I'm sorry, sweetheart," Linnea said.

Sally stared at her hand. "What the hell? I can't feel my fingers." Her eyes widened and she turned on Artemis. "What did you *do*?"

"What needed to be done," Artemis said.

Sally tried to stand up but her legs failed her and she fell back down on the couch. "No," she said. "No, no, no…"

Linnea put her arms around her sister and pulled her close. "Come here. It's okay, sweetheart. Just go to sleep. Go to sleep."

Sally made a quiet wailing noise and pushed against her sister, but she no longer had the strength to fight. A moment later she was asleep. Linnea stroked her back, tears now running down her face as well. "I love you, Sal. I love you."

"You *drugged* her?" Oliver asked Artemis. "How? I never even saw you move."

Artemis held up a small plastic bag the size of a half-dollar. "Sleight of hand, Mr. Jones." She smiled grimly. "She is going to be very cross with me when she wakes up."

Linnea laid her sister back on the couch and stroked her hair. "You'll take care of her?" she asked Artemis.

"Of course."

Linnea took a ragged breath and rubbed a tear from one eye. "Thank you. I never would have had a chance to say goodbye if it weren't for you." She kissed Sally on the cheek. "I love you, sweetheart."

"The bombing hasn't happened yet," Tyler said. "There's a chance, isn't there?" He looked at Artemis. "If she gets in and gets out, she could still live, right?"

Artemis sighed. "No."

"At least you're honest," Linnea said. She took a deep breath. "Gods. I'm so scared."

"Honesty compels me to be explicit with you," Artemis

said. "Transmit the cure, and the cyborgs will be cured. They will be made human again. But you will die. Nothing can save you."

"Maybe you didn't have to be *that* honest," Linnea said. She chuckled ruefully. "It's tempting, you know? I could just run away. Take Sal and get out of here."

"You could," Artemis said. "I would not prevent you. I cannot imagine you would last very long, though. The war is in its final stages, as you are well aware."

"Yeah." Linnea stood up and Oliver saw that one of her legs was trembling. She put a hand on her thigh until it stopped. "Well, I guess I have to go save the world."

"You are very brave, Linnea," Artemis said. "I always admired you. I would have you know that."

"Thanks. I always thought you were...very unusual."

"I am that."

Linnea looked at Tyler. "Take care of yourself, big guy. It was good to see you again." She looked at Oliver. "And you...I guess you're okay. Keep an eye on my sister for me. She's going to be so wrecked after this. She's going to need a lot of help."

"I will," Oliver said. "I promise."

"You may take our vehicle," Artemis said. "We will no longer have need of it."

Linnea nodded and headed for the door. A moment later Oliver heard their car start, and then it was gone.

"I believe we will have need of those handcuffs," Artemis said. "Before she wakes up, please, Mr. Jacobsen."

Tyler took the handcuffs and fastened Sally's hands behind her back. "Do we really have to do this?" he asked.

"Oh, yes. If she wakes up and kills the three of us in order to go after her sister, this trip will have been for nothing. Wouldn't you agree, Mr. Jones?"

"You didn't tell her," Oliver said.

"Hmm?"

"You told her she was going to cure the cyborgs. You never told her Sally would kill them afterward."

"No," Artemis said. "I did not. Do you disagree with my choice?"

Oliver shook his head. "You know what? I don't know what to think about anything, anymore. But honestly, screw this entire situation."

"Well, that is one perspective," Artemis said.

"What do we do now?" Tyler asked.

"We wait," Artemis said. The ground below them rumbled for a brief moment, then stopped. Artemis nodded. "It has begun."

Chapter 21

The second timequake came an hour later. It was larger this time, and lasted longer than the first one. The rumbling was enough to rouse Sally into groggy consciousness. "What did you do?" she asked, squinting as if the already dim light in the room was too bright for her.

"What needed to be done," Artemis said. "I apologize for the restraints, but I did not entertain the notion that any of us were a match for you, physically, and I could not risk you interfering."

Sally looked around. "Where's my sister?"

"She has gone to meet her destiny."

"My god," Oliver said. "Could you possibly sound any colder?"

Artemis turned to him. "Have I offended you, Mr. Jones? I have said nothing that is untrue. We must each meet our destiny, in our own time."

Sally tested the cuffs binding her wrists. "Let me go. I can still save her."

"You cannot," Artemis said. "It is too late. What is done is done. What happened before is now happening again."

"And we're talking in riddles now," Tyler said. "Fantastic."

"I did not hear a riddle," Artemis noted.

Sally glared at Artemis. "She's my sister!" She looked at Oliver and Tyler, and then back at Artemis. "Let me go. Artemis, I promise I'll let her finish the cure and then I'll get her out. We don't know when the attack is coming. I'll take the risk."

"I will not. The cyborgs have been searching for your sister for some time. It was her transmission of the cure program that allowed them to identify her location. Their missiles struck three minutes later. If you went there, you would only die with her. She, of course, was well aware of the danger she was in."

"*What*? You never told me any of that!"

"There was little reason to. In hindsight, perhaps I should have. If you had known how important the cure was to her, perhaps you would not have reacted to her death in the manner you did."

Sally looked around, her eyes frantic. "If you won't let me save her, at least keep me from deploying the weapon. You can do that much, can't you?"

"Of course not."

"Artemis…" Oliver began.

"Are you fucking kidding me?" Sally interrupted. "You don't have to uncuff me. Just go talk to the me at Federation

Command. Two versions of you yelling at me will be enough to stop me. Bring Tyler. Explain what happened."

Artemis sighed. "In a short time, my other self will implore you not to seek revenge. I remember that conversation quite clearly. You chose not to heed my advice. You will make the same choice again."

"But I didn't know then what I do now!"

"What is it that you know now, Sally?"

Sally's bottom lip trembled. "Damn it, Artemis, I was wrong! Is that what you want to hear? I thought it was justice, but it was just murder! I murdered all those people!" She looked at Oliver. "You know I'm right, don't you?"

As much as he didn't want to speak, Oliver nodded anyway. "Yes. I'm sorry, Sally, but it wasn't justice."

"There," Sally said. "See, Artemis? Isn't he your moral compass these days? You can stop this!"

The ground rumbled around them for the third time, and this time Oliver felt his chair rattling. "Unfortunately," Artemis said, "that is also a thing that cannot be changed."

"*What?*"

"It is what happened," Artemis said. "It is done. We cannot change the past."

"I think I'm proof that we can," Sally said.

"You are proof of how destructive such an endeavor can be."

"But it doesn't have to be like that," Sally said desperately. "So what if the cyborgs survive? The war will be over. Your world won't be invaded."

"But the timeline of my world would shatter," the girl said. "Even I cannot predict how destructive that could be. When you asked me to help you, I agreed. But I told you that if need be, I would burn your world to cinders in order to save my own. That world is my first responsibility."

"You mean you actually could save everyone?" Tyler asked.

"The timequakes indicate that I did not," Artemis said.

"But you could have?" Oliver asked. "And all it means is Sally never went back to Earth?"

"How many times has Sally saved your life, Mr. Jones? Or yours, Mr. Jacobsen? If she had not been exiled to our world, you would both likely be dead. And you are small things, compared to some of the larger pieces on the board."

"But all those people…" Sally said.

"They are already dead," Artemis said quietly. "They have been dead for a long time. If you had listened to me, perhaps they would not be. My own world's path would have been different. But you did not. You did not listen."

"And now you're punishing me for that?" Sally asked.

"I am not so petty as that," Artemis scoffed. "I am putting the history of our two worlds back the way it was supposed to be. And given that the ground is still shaking, and my headache has finally gone away, I can conclude that I was successful."

Sally thrashed against her handcuffs. "You crazy bitch!" she screamed. "I'll fucking kill you for this!"

"Perhaps you will," Artemis noted. "But you will not do it today." She looked around and took a last sip of her cold tea, grimacing at the taste. "This is the final timequake. It is done."

"Do we need to get back to the mirror or something?" Tyler asked.

"Of course not." She turned to watch as the house's windows began to crack from the increased shaking. "We were never here."

And then the world went black.

Chapter 22

Oliver woke up on his couch with a nasty hangover, Jeffrey sleeping next to him. The DVD menu for *Back to the Future* was playing on the television on endless repeat, waiting for someone to either start the movie or enjoy its variety of special features. It would play until the end of time, or at least until someone shut the power off.

Oliver squinted against the light that was streaming in from his living room window. His mouth tasted like he'd been chewing on a dirty sock. What time was it?

He reached out and scratched Jeffrey's back, causing the cat to stretch out and yawn.

Memories battled in Oliver's head as if trying to assert their dominance. Sally had been here last night, hadn't she? They'd watched movies and had too many margaritas. He suspected she'd put something in his drink, something just strong enough to get his mind wandering. She'd been trying to get him to believe they had access to a working time machine. It had been important to her that he believed it. And he *had* believed it.

He'd repaired the damn thing, albeit unwittingly. If it was still there, Oliver resolved to go down to the vault and smash it to bits with a sledgehammer.

Oliver stood up and went to look out his window. He almost expected to see cyborgs outside, patrolling on the sidewalk in front of his house. Instead he saw nothing more interesting than a man walking his dog. It was still somewhat foggy out, but it looked as if that would burn off in an hour or two. It was going to be a beautiful day.

Jeffrey stirred on the couch. "I feel awful," the cat said. Oliver went over and sat down next to him, reaching out to massage the scruff of his neck.

"What do you remember?" Oliver asked.

The cat crawled his way onto Oliver's lap and curled up. "There were cyborgs, and I was all alone, but your friends found me and took me to that crazy house where time is weird, but then I could remember things and talk again. And you came, and you dressed up like a cyborg so nobody could tell you were sneaking around." The cat opened his eyes. "I waited for you, but then things changed and I woke up here just now. Is everything okay now?"

Oliver sighed. "I think so. I keep expecting something to happen, like that one cyborg is going to come in and make me eat nutrient paste for breakfast." That cyborg had had a name, hadn't he? No, he'd had a *designation*. SCI…something or other. Oliver found he was having trouble remembering parts of what had happened, as if it were a slowly-fading dream.

"But it's not going to happen, is it?" Jeffrey looked up at him. "Let's stay here, and you can cook me some sausages, and we'll watch *Star Trek* all day."

"As long as we skip the episodes that have time travel and other dimensions," Oliver said. "I think I'm done with those subjects."

"Good. I like this world better. And I can talk and think about things, which is pretty good."

"Yeah." Oliver rubbed his eyes. "I think I'd better go to work, though."

"Do you have to?"

Oliver considered it. "I do today," he said. "Tomorrow I might get my resume out and start looking for a new job. Something nice and boring."

"Really?"

"I guess we'll see."

Oliver took the train into the financial district, unsure if he was in any condition to drive. He had a few bouts of intermittent dizziness and once was almost certain he spotted a cyborg patrol, but it was gone when he took a second look. He wanted very much to go home and go back to bed, but decided he could sleep later. Right now he needed some answers.

Bruce looked up at him as he entered the office's lobby. "Good morning, sunshine," he called from the reception desk.

"Hi," Oliver said. He realized he had no idea what had happened to Bruce in the other timeline. He'd probably been killed or converted in the initial invasion. "How are you this morning?"

"Can't complain. Artemis wants to see you first thing."

Oliver watched the other man for a moment, trying to size him up, but Bruce appeared to be his normal chipper self. He'd never been to the house on Filbert Street, Oliver realized. From his perspective, nothing out of the ordinary had happened. "I guess I'll get in there, then."

"That's sure what *I'd* do," Bruce said.

Seven rushed past Oliver in the hallway, heading for his lab. Oliver was about to stop the other man and ask how he was coping, but then realized Seven had never made it to the house on Filbert Street, either. He'd be completely unaware of the other timeline, and the fact that he'd died in it. There didn't seem to be much point in telling him about it. Seven would just think he'd gone nuts. Or worse, he'd believe every word of it.

Artemis was behind her desk when Oliver stepped into her office, her customary pot of tea sitting on her desk. "Close the door," she said.

Oliver shut the door and took one of the chairs in front of her desk. "Tea?" Artemis asked.

"I'm not in the mood for tea," Oliver said.

"Ah, yes. Sally got you drunk the night before she took the time machine. I imagine you are feeling a bit under the weather."

"Something like that."

Artemis nodded. "I have spoken with Maria this morning. She is well, and sends her thanks. So, Mr. Jones. How are you?"

Oliver resisted the urge to say *fine*. Artemis never made small talk, and he was in no mood for it, anyway. "The other timeline feels like a dream. Parts of it are slipping away. Just the small details, I guess. I remember the important things."

Artemis nodded. "That was to be expected. Certain things will fade away entirely, but you will remember the larger matters. You may find yourself experiencing a form of post-traumatic stress. I am unfamiliar with how that feels, having never experienced it myself, but it is not uncommon for my employees to seek relief in therapy. We have someone you can speak with, if you feel it necessary. She is cleared to hear things that others may not."

"Why am I not surprised the company has a therapist?"

"It was not always so. We are a progressive company."

"Was that a joke?" Oliver asked.

"Not entirely, Mr. Jones. It was more of a statement that things change."

"Not everything."

"No, I suppose not. Are you certain you won't have tea?"

"I don't want any tea."

"Then you should get to work. I require you to visit Vault 3 and conduct an inspection. I would not expect that anything has been disturbed now that the timeline has been restored, but I do dislike surprises."

Oliver nodded. "Where's Tyler?"

"Tyler is not feeling well, and has taken the day off. I will not ask you to take Seven, for obvious reasons. I believe he already suspects there was a timeline fracture, but I will deal with that in time. For today, I would prefer not to have to tell him he was killed. He will not sleep for days once I do."

"Yeah," Oliver said. "And what about Sally?"

Artemis sipped her tea. "Sally is no longer with the company."

Oliver felt a chill run down his spine. "What does that mean, exactly?"

"It means precisely what I said, Mr. Jones. She is gone. Surely it is not your concern."

"It's very much my concern," Oliver said. He heard an edge in his voice that surprised him a little, but given the circumstances, he felt it was justified. "She's my friend."

"Is she?" Artemis raised an eyebrow. "I seem to recall a short time ago you were not certain you could continue working with her, so concerned were you with her monstrous past."

Oliver felt himself getting angry. *No*, he realized. He was getting *angrier*. "I swear to god, if you killed her…"

"Of course I did not kill her, Mr. Jones. She is one of my people, after all. I am not in the habit of killing you. And before you ask, neither did anybody else. She is alive and well."

"Then where is she?"

"Somewhere she is safe and comfortable, and no longer a threat to herself or anyone else."

Oliver wondered if Artemis would even notice if he punched her in the face, or if she'd just go on talking like a robot as if nothing had happened. "You sent her to the island, didn't you? Wherever that is. So she's sitting in a damn cell?"

Artemis sighed. "She is not in a cell, other than in the sense that the island itself is a cell from which she cannot escape."

"She made a mistake, damn it…"

"She made quite a series of mistakes, Mr. Jones. She annihilated the cyborgs after they had been rendered harmless in a childish attempt to avenge her sister."

"She tried to fix that…"

"By altering time, which was an even bigger mistake. The past *cannot* be changed, Mr. Jones. There is nothing more dangerous. As unpleasant as it may be, we are forced to live with the consequences of the things we have done. If we know we have done wrong, our only option is to attempt to do better in the future. Sally did not do that."

"You think she doesn't know she was wrong by now?"

"I think she cannot be controlled, and that she is far too clever and resourceful to remain at liberty. I cannot imagine what she would try next, and I am not willing to find out. Hence, she will live out her days on the island. Put her from your mind."

Oliver stood up, fists clenched. "Put her from my mind? Are you kidding me?"

"I was not."

"Do you have any feelings at all, you crazy little bitch? Does *anything* bother you? What was it you said before? We're just small pieces, compared to some of the larger ones on the board? We're just pawns to you, aren't we?" Oliver realized he was shouting, something he hadn't done in a very long time. He was surprised to find that he didn't care. "Our little lives mean nothing to you. You sit there in your high chair and tell us what to do, and the minute we're gone you don't even remember us. Sally would have *died* for you!"

Artemis stared at him with eyes of ice. Oliver wondered for

a moment if he'd just bought himself a ticket to the island as well, but it didn't matter anymore. Good luck to her if she tried anything. He wasn't going down without a fight.

Artemis took a deep breath. "Do I have feelings, Mr. Jones?" she asked quietly. "Do I? I have been doing this for longer than you can possibly imagine. I have lost more…I have lost every single person I have ever cared for, and it hurts me every day. I feel that loss every waking moment. And since you asked, I remember *all* of you."

They stared at each other for a moment longer, neither of them blinking, until Artemis finally looked away. "I remember all of you," she repeated softly, and for the first time since he'd known her Oliver heard sorrow in her voice. "Get out of my office, Mr. Jones. You may return to work tomorrow, or you may do…you may do whatsoever you may wish. Regardless, I will remember you until the day I finally leave this Earth." She swung her chair around so she was facing the wall and said no more.

Oliver hesitated, wanting to say something else, but the words wouldn't come. He turned and left the office, shutting the door behind him.

Chapter 23

Oliver stood on the sidewalk outside the office for a good five minutes, feeling like he wanted to punch a wall, but also realizing that he'd both look stupid to passersby and probably break his hand. Around him cars drove along and pedestrians went about their business, oblivious to the fact that in another timeline they'd all be dead or walking around in cyborg armor. If he told them, they'd just think he was a crazy person. Maybe that explained some of the crazy people he saw ranting on the streets at times. Maybe they weren't actually crazy; they just knew something nobody else did.

Oliver took out his cell phone and called Tyler. The other man answered on the third ring. "You okay?" Tyler's voice was groggy and slightly slurred. He sounded like he was well into a bottle of Scotch.

"You know what happened to Sally?"

"I don't want to talk about it."

"Tyler…"

"I said I don't want to talk about it. Leave me alone."

Oliver sighed. "Fine. We can talk about it later. Are you all right?"

"No. I'm hanging up now. See you tomorrow." The connection dropped.

Oliver looked at his phone for a moment, not sure what to do next. He really had nobody else to call. Who was he going to tell about any of this? Who wouldn't tell him to go see a psychiatrist and get on some medication to make the crazy go away? After another minute, he stuck the phone in his pocket and headed for the train station. Going home and sleeping for the rest of the day sounded like a pretty good plan.

He was nearly to the station at Embarcadero when he spotted someone he recognized, a girl in her late teens with long blonde hair. Today she wore an ill-fitting purple suit that had obviously been made for a man, along with a green vest and a tie to complete the outfit. The clothes looked vaguely familiar, but Oliver wasn't sure from where. That was the least of his worries, though. The fact that he was seeing the girl at all was strange. She was the one who had been skipping along with the cyborg patrol back in Russian Hill, back when he and Tyler had gone to steal a Humvee. The cyborgs either hadn't noticed her presence or just didn't care, but neither of those things seemed very likely. Tyler hadn't been able to see her, either, he remembered. The girl had clearly seen Oliver, though. At the time she'd waved merrily at him.

She spotted him again now and walked over to where he stood, smiling broadly. "Do you think I'm pretty?" she asked.

"Who are you?"

"Oh, I'm doing the *Joker*," she said. "I wasn't quite finished with the costume, though." She ran her fingers through her blonde hair, which turned dark green at the touch. Then she rubbed her head with both hands to mess it up. "I might do the makeup, too, but I haven't decided yet. I don't like to cover my face."

There would have been a time when Oliver would have been so startled by this turn of events that he'd either have been rendered speechless or just run away, but he was no longer that person. "I didn't mean the costume," he said. "I meant who are you?"

The girl pouted. "You really don't recognize me yet?" she asked. She searched his face. "No, you don't. Now that you're finally waking up, you will soon enough. I don't want to ruin the fun for you."

"Why couldn't the cyborgs see you in the other timeline?"

"Oh, that's right," the girl said. "I almost forgot you saw me over there. I was going to come and say hello, but I was having *such* a good time. True chaos is so rare these days, and a whole broken timeline? That was just…" she sighed lustily, "*exquisite.*"

Oliver had thought his frustration couldn't have gotten any worse after his confrontation with Artemis, but it turned out that hadn't been the case at all. "You know what?" he asked. "I don't have time for this." He turned to go.

"Aw," the girl said. "I know. You're having a bad day. Poor Sally Rain. She was one of mine, if only for a little while. And now she's all alone on that island." The girl bit her lip. "Well, she's not really *alone*. There are other things there, too. But nobody for her to talk to. Even the monsters that are smart enough to have figured out language don't really have anything to say."

"How do you know about her? How do you know about any of that?"

The girl sighed, then stood on tiptoe to kiss him on the cheek. "I missed you so much," she whispered into his ear. "I really did. You were always my favorite brother."

Oliver stared at her in shock. "*Brother*? You're wrong, I don't have any…" Oliver was an only child. He didn't even have any cousins that he knew of. "You've mistaken me for someone else."

She grinned at him. "No, I haven't. It took me so long to find you, big brother, but I finally did. Now we'll just have to see what happens next." She rubbed her hands together eagerly and Oliver saw a glint in her eyes. "Maybe a family reunion? Now *that* would be chaos." She laughed merrily. "But it won't be today. You're not quite there yet. You can't even remember who you are!" She turned to go. "Oh, say hi to Jeffrey for me." She giggled. "A talking cat! That's so perfect! Maybe I'll get one, too." She skipped away from Oliver and was lost in the crowd a few seconds later.

It occurred to Oliver that he'd failed to ask what she meant when she said he was finally waking up, but that opportunity was gone. But all things considered, on the list of unusual things that had happened to him in the last six months, this encounter wouldn't even have rated in the top ten. Still, the girl had known about Sally Rain and Jeffrey. He suspected he'd see her again soon. Maybe next time she'd be a little more willing to answer some questions.

Oliver looked at the sky. The morning fog had burned off

and the sun was bright overhead. The world had moved on without a care. He decided he was done thinking about his interesting life for now. Maybe he'd take Jeffrey for a walk down by the water. The cat would enjoy that. Or maybe he'd just go to bed. But no matter what, he was taking the rest of the day off. He could deal with his problems tomorrow. Nothing at all strange was going to happen today. It just wasn't *allowed* to.

But of course that wasn't how things worked out. It wasn't even close.

ALSO BY MATTHEW STORM

The Interesting Times Series

Interesting Times
Interesting Places
Interesting People

Nevada James Mysteries

Broken
Scars

The Riley Flynn Series (as M.J. Storm)

Riley Flynn and the Runaway Fairy

ABOUT THE AUTHOR

Matthew Storm lives in Anchorage, Alaska. He may or may not have a time machine. It's not as if you'd know the difference, anyway.